Harley wasn't sure she'd heard him right.

"You want me to take off my clothes?"

He nodded.

"Here?"

He nodded.

"Now?"

He nodded. It was all he could manage with Harley not ten feet away. Damn, but reality beat the pants off phone calls. "Do you need some help?"

"Do you want to help?"

"No," he croaked, making fists of both hands. "I'll watch."

"All right," she whispered, then shrugged and her blouse slid from one shoulder, then the other. Sliding down her arms. Catching on her wrists. Hitting the floor with a sigh that Gardner echoed at the first sight of her breasts.

Dear Reader,

Nothing beats the thrill of being in the right place at the right time. How about driving past your dream house when the For Sale sign goes up in the yard? Or promising to start your diet tomorrow, then stopping for ice cream and meeting your fantasy man in front of the freezer?

How about having your manuscript at a publishing house in the hands of the senior editor of the line for which you want to write the very moment *that* house, *that* editor and *that* line have been selected to be profiled on national television?

Call it fate. Call it luck. Call it serendipity. Any of the three could be applied to the selection of *Call Me* as the manuscript contracted live on CBS "48 Hours." No one could have been more surprised than I to receive the call from the show's producer.

The call from Birgit Davis-Todd would have come with or without the show, though I was thrilled at the way things turned out. The timing and circumstances allowed so many old and new friends to share the experience with me.

But don't credit fate, luck or serendipity for the story you are about to read. The words you'll find on these pages are the result of my love for true romance and Harlequin Temptation.

Yours sincerely,

Alison Kent

P.S. Please write to me c/o Harlequin, 225 Duncan Mill Road, Don Mills, Ontario, Canada M3B 3K9

CALL ME
Alison Kent

Harlequin Books

TORONTO • NEW YORK • LONDON
AMSTERDAM • PARIS • SYDNEY • HAMBURG
STOCKHOLM • ATHENS • TOKYO • MILAN
MADRID • WARSAW • BUDAPEST • AUCKLAND

To the editors who applauded my manuscript's first baby steps
and continued to provide the guidance, nurturing and
megadoses of encouragement that sent this story soaring:
Laura Shin, Brenda Chin, Birgit Davis-Todd, Susan Sheppard.
A special thank-you to the CBS "48 Hours" crew who provided
me the means to enjoy this sale over and over—at least until the
videotape wears out.
Most of all, to Jan, for the words and the pictures.
Thank you, friend.

ISBN 0-373-25694-9

CALL ME

Copyright © 1996 by Mica Kelch.

Printed in U.S.A.

1

It's up to you.

"IT'S UP TO YOU." Mona Tedrick frowned at the cryptic message scrawled on the back of the business card. She flicked the white rectangle like the filter end of a cigarette and repeated, "It's up to you? That's it? Nothing else?"

Reaching across the corner of her rolltop desk, Harley Golden plucked the card from her shop assistant's hand. She wasn't about to risk damage to a piece of paper that was her only connection to the man of her dreams.

A man she'd seen once. A man she would never see again.

"Yes, that's it. No, there's nothing else." *And since it's up to me, that's that.* Stroking her thumb over the bold raised letters, she slid the black-and-white souvenir of her fantasy under the corner of her desk blotter. With the memento out of sight, she released a weighty sigh, picked up her number-two pencil and squinted down at the estate sale invoice.

She really did need to think about computerizing her customer accounts the same way she had her shop inventory. It didn't make good business sense to keep her clients' idiosyncratic preferences filed away in her head.

But keeping the books in old-fashioned green ledgers just seemed so simpatico with her old-fashioned surroundings. Besides, her hands-on accounting method complemented the personal service she'd offered her customers since opening Golden's Touch.

"You've already decided not to call him, haven't you?"

Harley continued writing. "C'mon, Mona. I'm not the flake he obviously mistook me for. How many women do you think he pulls this 'call-me' routine on?"

Checking her reflection in the cheval glass behind Harley's desk, Mona smoothed her diagonally slashed hair from earlobe to chin. "Who cares? If this guy's the *Playgirl* material you say he is, I'd go for it."

"The guy was stuffed like a sausage in the seat of a 727." Harley recorded the invoice total in Mrs. Mitchmore's account, slammed the ledger and tossed her pencil on top. "So he had a nice face. Even *Playgirl* would need to know more than that before pursuing the man."

Mona jackknifed her long legs into the me 's easy chair she'd pulled up next to Harley's desk. A pensive look creased her brows into a dark V. "When you say sausage, do you mean Vienna? Jumbo frank?"

Harley glared.

"Polish link?"

"What I mean is that airline seats were not designed with the human body in mind. If Mrs. Mitchmore isn't satisfied with the blanket chest, then the next estate sale I hit I'm flying first-class and tacking it on to her bill."

"Which is exactly what Mrs. Mitchmore has told you to do since the beginning of time," Mona reminded Harley.

"True."

"But you won't, because traveling first-class makes you feel like you're taking advantage of your clients."

"True, again."

"And being the Miss Goody-Two-Shoes that you are, you choose to suffer for the cause because it balances out the guilt you feel for enjoying what you do."

"True for the third time." Harley kicked off her taupe heels, flexed her toes and groaned. "Speaking of shoes, I've got to pick up a new pair in the morning. Something with cushioned heels. And soles. And toes. I'm going to be shopping most of tomorrow and my feet are hamburger."

Mona dismissed tomorrow with a wave of her elegant fingers. "You've been back two hours from a two-day buying trip. Take tomorrow off. I can handle a Saturday on my own."

Harley didn't have a doubt. She'd recruited the flamboyant arts major from an exclusive gallery where Mona's dramatic flare for setup and design had often outclassed artists' showings.

Here at Golden's Touch, Mona's eccentric eye for detail was responsible for more than one customer's return visit. And that's why Harley paid Mona close to what she paid herself.

"Much as I'd like to kick back tomorrow, I can't. I had a message on the answering machine. A patient of Dr. Fischer's insists she saw a Shaker syrup bottle in one of the antique stores in Spring. The good doctor sounded desperate."

"The good doctor always sounds desperate."

"Which is why I'm determined to finish both his office and his study before Christmas. That gives me two and a half months to finish the job. It's a good commission, but what he's costing me isn't worth what he's paying me."

"Tell him you need more."

"What I need is to be done with this job."

Mona reached up to switch on Harley's Tiffany desk lamp, then pulled the business card from beneath the blotter. "Enough already about business. Tell me about this guy."

Harley breathed deep. It was time to deal with the fantasy and put it to bed. "There's not much to say. The guy was gorgeous. End of discussion."

Mona blinked. "Oh. How stupid of me. I forgot. Harley Golden doesn't do gorgeous guys."

"Give me brains over beauty and brawn any day."

"Harley," Mona admonished. "You've got to quit judging every potential hunk by your ex. Just because Brad had abs and buns of steel, plus that other hard part that got him into trouble, doesn't mean all hunks are scum."

Harley stashed the ledger in a desk drawer, slamming it shut. "I don't want to talk about Brad."

"Why not? Ever since your divorce, the only men you talk about are René Lalique, Louis Tiffany and Thomas Chippendale."

"At least they don't moan to me about their therapist, their mother or their Pekingese." And they sure as hell don't sleep around, Harley couldn't help but mentally add.

"Pekingese, huh? You must be talking about Sahara."

"Admit it," Harley said, pinning her friend with a pained look. "The guys you fix me up with are weird."

Mona stuck her nose in the air. "My friends are not weird."

"Okay. Then they're just not my type."

"Was the mysterious Mr. Business Card your type?"

"Yes. No. I told you. He was too good-looking."

"So, then, why the major eye contact on the flight?"

"He started it."

"Which gives you the upper hand. He wants you. And doesn't know a thing about you. Call him. Create a new identity. Have phone sex."

"Mona!" Harley gasped, outraged.

"Do something wild and scandalous, Harley, before you become as fossilized as this room of antiques."

"I'm not old enough to be an antique."

"You're one-third of the way there."

"I'm ignoring you, Mona." Frowning, Harley pulled her organizer from her briefcase. Knowing she'd never decipher Mona's scrawl, she handed over the stack of message slips sitting beneath her paperweight. "Give me the rundown on who's called about what since I left Wednesday."

Mona covered the half-dozen or so requests and Harley jotted notes. "I can probably knock out two or three of these tomorrow."

"And then what?"

"What do you mean 'and then what'?" Harley asked.

Mona expelled a theatrical sigh. "I can't believe I'm saying this, but there's more to a woman's life than shopping, Harley Golden."

"That coming from you? Anyway, this kind of shopping is the best of all. I get to spend obscene amounts of other people's money on totally extravagant items." She wiggled her brows. "And they pay me to do it."

"Oooh. Thrill me to death. Harley, do you realize when Gibson and I picked you up last Saturday night you were still in the shop?"

Harley's chair squeaked as she crossed one leg beneath her. "Of course I was. I live here."

"No, you live upstairs. You were down here. In the shop. Working."

"Saturday evenings are closure time for me. You know, updating the books and the customer files, rearranging displays to compensate for items sold." She shrugged. "That leaves me Sunday free to do what I want."

"So what do you do on Sundays?" Mona held up one hand. "No, wait. Let me guess. You go through all the trade papers, making lists of which antique auctions and estate sales you can hit the next week. Harley, get a life!"

"Fine," Harley grumbled, knowing there was but one way to shut up her assistant. She flipped to the address section of her organizer and ran her pencil down every page. She was up to the letter *S* before she realized she wasn't going to find a date in here. She hadn't made many male acquaintances since her divorce. Her fault, really. She hadn't been in the mood.

She'd thrown herself into her business, wanting to validate her own self-worth. To prove that it wasn't something inside her that had driven Brad to other women.

She shut the organizer. "Okay, who was that guy you and Gibson fixed me up with?"

"Which one?"

"Remember? The four of us did the museum thing. Omri. He wasn't too bad." Harley picked up her pencil. "What's his number?"

"Omri. Hmmm." Mona examined the lacquer on her nails. "Not a good idea."

"Why not?"

"He's in Tibet."

"Tibet?"

"He's entering the monastery."

Harley tossed her pencil in the air. "Great. I drove the man to a life of celibacy."

"I don't think you had a lot to do with it."

"You're probably right. He did spend the evening praising the Dalai Lama." Harley sighed. "Too much competition for me."

"That's just it." Mona leaned forward, her face expressive. "You don't have to compete. You're stunning. When are you going to realize it?"

Harley glanced from Mona's dramatic black hair and ruby lips to her own reflection in the mirror. Tucked beneath the navy-and-taupe designer suit was a body that wasn't half-bad. But unlike a certain unnamed assistant, Harley wasn't one to flaunt.

As far as makeup went, well, her eyes were already a huge sleepy-looking blue. If she added anything more than a coat of mascara, she resembled a three-year-old who'd gotten into her mother's cosmetics. And the bow of her mouth was so plump that applying lipstick gave her the look of a forties' starlet.

Her hair was hopeless. Wheat-colored wisps escaped from the topknot she'd tucked it in. She shook her head and the strands tumbled to her shoulders in a heavy mass of fifteen different blondes. Her dimples weren't a bad touch, but she looked like the Keebler elf when she smiled. She glanced back at Mona.

The other woman's jet black brow arched. "Well? What do you think?"

"Okay, I guess." She finger-combed her hair from her forehead. "I just don't like to fuss."

"Judging by this business-card business, you don't need to."

"Can we forget this business-card business? Please?"

"Are you kidding? C'mon. Tell me everything. Start with what he looked like."

It was no use. Mona would never give up. "He was wearing a classic Italian suit. His hair was short." Harley gestured above her ears. "Not military-style, but that precision model cut. It was dark...but not as dark as his lashes. They were spiky. And long. And his eyes. Hmmm. An incredible icy green." Harley shivered and sighed. "He was very... continental. And entirely too scrumptious for me."

Mona tapped a wine-dark nail on the arm of her chair. "He sounds perfect. When are you going to call?"

"Never. I spent four years married to a man too gorgeous for his own good—and for mine. Brad spent so much time admiring himself and getting up close and personal with his exercise groupies that he forgot he had a wife."

Harley shook her head. "No more studs for me, thank you very much. I want a man who knows how to treat a woman." She pounded her fist on her desk.

"I want attention. I want worship. I want my man to drool at my feet."

"Maybe you'd better get a dog."

"Exactly my point. I'll never find what I want because I'm too picky to settle for less."

Mona pushed up out of her chair, smoothing down the mandarin collar of her dramatic black tunic. "Well, I'm off. It's Friday night and Gibson has promised me candlelight, wine and shrimp Florentine at his place."

Harley got to her feet, laid her arm across Mona's shoulders and walked her friend to the door. "Have a good time for me, too."

"If I make up for what you've been missing, you won't see me for months."

"Very funny," Harley mumbled, but Mona was already halfway down the block.

Lowering the front window's lace-and-linen shade, Harley flipped the sign to Closed and wandered back through the store. She swept her palm over the smoothness of a refinished oak chiffonier, lingered on the lavishly carved details of a carousel horse and fingered an iridescent carnival glass punch bowl before returning to her desk and the more mundane tasks of running Golden's Touch.

The mundane no longer held any appeal. All Mona's talk of men and fun had sparked to life a restlessness Harley was finding difficult to keep tamped down. She wished she had an ounce of Mona's boldness when it came to relationships. But Brad's infidelity had made her wary of involvement.

No, that wasn't exactly true. Her wariness had much deeper and more personal roots than an unfaithful husband. It had started years before, once she'd been old enough to realize that her parents' love for each other wasn't normal. Or healthy.

What it was was obsessive. Smothering. Consuming. And that destructive emotion had frightened her more than the times early in her childhood when Buck and Trixie had left Harley and her sister home alone for days.

She'd vowed years later to never settle for less than pure and perfect love. A love founded in mutual respect, and seasoned through time with friendship and passion.

Brad had happened along during one of her weaker moments.

The first time he'd asked her out, her sorority sisters at the University of Texas had shrieked with envy. Later she'd come to realize it was her lack of big Texas hair and her fresh farm-girl face that appealed to Brad. When they were together, he received the attention. But she'd been blindly enamored, and young, and naive enough to believe he'd grow to love her with the same intensity.

She'd still believed it four years later when she'd found him in bed with one of her sorority sisters who'd had a layover in Houston. Brad had moved out as Harley had asked, giving her time to reconcile her feelings.

Catching him in the parking lot of his health spa with one of the club bunnies, who notched hard bodies on her bedpost, cinched Harley's decision.

She'd thrown herself into her business then—a business Brad had never been crazy about. Easy enough to understand. When he'd walked through the shop he'd been outshined by the beauty of aged wood, beveled glass, etched crystal and gold.

Harley glanced around at the merchandise she offered, every piece with a history of its own. *Mona's right,* Harley thought. *I'm petrifying. A quick stain and varnish and I'll blend right in.* It was pretty pathetic that a thirty-year-old woman got her thrills from a Louis XV instead of a flesh-and-blood Louis.

She wasn't a total hermit. She did go out. And she wasn't afraid to take risks. Every time she accepted one of Mona's fix-ups she was taking a big one. Mona and her friends existed on a plane that belonged in a whole other dimension.

A monk. Good grief.

Harley picked up the business card.

Gardner Barnes
Excalibur's King of Prince William's Knight
915-555-1782

A risk? A thrill? Or sheer stupidity? Whichever, she picked up the phone and punched in the number.

She wanted to hear his voice one more time. An experiment to test what she was sure she'd imagined. The tingle at her nape, the dampness behind her knees, the tightness in her lungs.

The connection clicked at the fourth ring, stopping Harley's heart.

"Yo. Stud Central."

GARDNER CROSSED BEHIND his uncle Judson, stepped over a kitchen chair pulled out from the table and grabbed the receiver from Ty's hand. "Hello?"

Hearing nothing but a dial tone, he cuffed his younger brother on the shoulder. "What the hell are you doing?"

Ty glared back. "You want to expand the operation of this ranch? Get yourself a secretary, Gardner. I'm tired of answering the damned phone."

"Look, Tyler. This breeding venture benefits you as much as anybody. You want a free ride to Texas A & M next fall, you answer the phone."

"It's not your breeding venture sending me to A & M, Gardner. It's those barrels of crude oil pumping out of Acre 52," Ty retorted. "The same West Texas Sour that paid for your Cessna."

Gardner grabbed a skillet of hamburger steaks from the stove and slammed it onto the table. "You just help your uncle get supper on. I'll call the men."

Spatula in hand, Judson stepped into his path. "Ain't no call getting riled at the boy, Gardner, just 'cuz you got a bee buzzing."

Hands on his hips, Gardner met his uncle's gaze, then turned back to his brother. "Sorry, Ty. It's been a bitch of a day."

Ty flashed his cocky eighteen-year-old grin. "Yeah, well, when you climbed out of the Cessna wearing a suit and tie, I figured you'd have my butt in a sling before the day was out."

Gardner glanced down at his scuffed boots and saddle-broke jeans. "I always take it out on you, don't I?"

"Only because me and Jud are the only kin you got."

"And he knows better than to take it out on me," Judson put in, upending a pan of corn-bread muffins before heading to the back porch to call the men.

Ty snatched a muffin from the platter. "C'mon, Gardner. Get yourself a wife. Or at least head up to Austin and get yourself a coed. They're better than aspirin for relieving aches and pains."

"Take two coeds and call me in the morning, huh? You been following your own advice, Dr. Barnes?" Ty colored. Gardner bit his cheek to keep from smiling. And Judson let out a guffaw just before the porch screen slammed shut.

The clang of the triangle signaled dinner—and the beginning of another very long, lonely Friday night. Leaving Tyler in the kitchen—half a corn-bread muffin in his mouth, another in his hand—Gardner stepped off the back porch of the farmhouse his family had lived in for four generations. He gave a passing wave to the eight cowboys headed from the barn to the house and headed in the opposite direction.

Crossing a yard of more dirt than sod, he gazed at the flat Texas grasslands he was proud to call his own. And standing front and center in the nearest pasture was his dream.

Excalibur's King of Prince William's Knight.

Judged by looks alone, the Beefmaster bull was one ugly son of a bitch. But as black tempered and mean spirited as he was, he did a hell of a job standing stud. His offspring were prime. He made it possible for Gardner to run Camelot the way a ranch ought to be run.

Camelot. Gardner blew out a puff of disgust. His father must've had his head in the clouds when he allowed his mother to rename the ranch. But Gardner Sr. had walked ten feet off the ground anytime Jean was around. That's why when she'd died, he'd followed six

months later, leaving twenty-two-year-old Gardner and
ten-year-old Ty a family legacy to carry into the next
generation.

So far Gardner hadn't found the time. Along with his
uncle Judson, he'd spent his life expanding the operation of Camelot and acting as surrogate father to Ty.
Neither left room for a personal life. Usually he didn't
mind.

Handing his card to that woman on the plane wasn't
his style. He'd been dozing, recouping from a morning
of meetings with his Dallas bankers, and on the way to
Houston for a business luncheon with the Texas con-
tingent of Beefmaster Breeders.

Glancing up at the attendant's offer of a drink, he'd
found himself staring across the aisle at wide bluebonnet eyes. She'd been summer in the morning, a long
winter's night and salvation at the end of a hard-
working day.

He'd watched the pure female motion of her fingers
as she'd shuffled her papers and gripped her pen, or
brushed stray wisps of hair from her face. He'd watched
the rise and fall of her breathing, the way she tugged at
her skirt when she twisted in her seat.

He'd seen her smile to herself, then glance up to see
if she'd been caught in the act. He'd witnessed her frown
when her paperwork displeased her, and her amuse-
ment when the child in front of her announced that he
couldn't wait until they landed—he had to go *now*.

And because Gardner couldn't neatly catalog his response, he'd looked closer. At the briefcase tucked beneath her seat, the paperwork spread across the tray
table, the suit that no doubt cost as much as his.

Still he'd looked. And she'd looked. He'd nodded a greeting. She'd done the same. He'd asked if she was stopping in Houston or catching a connecting flight. She'd revealed that Houston was home, then turned the question back to him.

He'd told her he was only in town for a meeting, and she'd said he'd picked a good month. October in Houston was perfect. She'd smiled briefly, then focused on the papers littering her table tray, as if embarrassed the conversation had so quickly regressed to the weather.

The plane had landed then. And for once in his life, Gardner made a decision without hours of thought backing it up. When she'd stepped into the aisle beside him, he'd pressed his card into her hand.

He shook his head, still unable to figure why he'd done what he did. A fool. That's what he was. A fool. Praying that she'd dropped his card in the first wastebasket she'd seen in the terminal, Gardner headed for the barn where he saddled his roan gelding, Merlin.

Two hours later, he entered a quiet house with no sign of Judson or Ty, took a long lukewarm shower and toweled his hair dry. Exhausted, he slid naked between the sheets. But he couldn't sleep.

He flopped over, his hearing alert, his heart beating so hard his throat ached. *Don't be an ass, Gardner. Sunup's in less than eight hours.* And since he'd drawn KP this week, he needed to be up in six.

He closed his eyes and breathed deep, ticking off the minutes in his mind. Thirty later, he turned onto his back and, grumbling under his breath, tossed off the sheet and tried again.

Another half hour passed before he determined he was in for a bout of insomnia. Swinging his feet to the floor, he figured he'd head downstairs to his study and get in a couple of hours' work on his breeding data base before he started breakfast.

The ring of the phone stopped him cold.

2

"HELLO?"

The male voice was gruff, slightly sleepy, and the timbre raised the hair on her arms. Harley hesitated a minute before exhaling a simple "Hi."

She cringed, and damned the breathlessness in her voice. She sounded like a woman calling for phone sex. Great. Mona would love it.

Swallowing dry air, she licked her parched lips and listened, hearing a long, satisfied sigh and the creak of . . . bedsprings.

"I was wondering if you'd call." His voice seeped through her, wickedly deep and low.

"I was wondering myself," she managed to answer.

"What made up your mind?"

Harley shrugged for her own benefit. How much did she want to tell him? And did she even know? "I think it was something about chances not taken."

"You take them a lot?"

"Almost never."

He chuckled, a resonant rumble. Pure male. Pure temptation. Harley curled her toes into the mattress, settled deeper between two pillows and pulled her sheet to her chin.

"Neither do I," he finally said.

She responded with, "Then why did you give me your card?"

She waited, anticipating his answer, wondering what he had seen in her that prompted his impulsive move.

"I'm not sure, but I think I'd like you to help me find out." He breathed into her ear.

Harley closed her eyes, opened them slowly. Trembling, she listened to the bedsprings again. Bedsprings. Uh-oh. What if he wasn't alone? "I'm sorry. Did I wake you?"

"No, I was up."

O . . . kay. "I forget Friday nights don't start at eleven for everyone. I shouldn't have called so late."

"Actually, I was just getting out of bed."

Why, because you're a love-'em-and-leave-'em kind of guy? "Uh, maybe this wasn't such a good idea."

"It's fine." He sounded almost desperate. "In fact, I've been thinking about you."

Did that mean he *was* alone? "I tried to call earlier, but got a wrong number."

"No. What you got was my brother," he said, sounding very pleased that she'd tried again.

"Your brother lives with you?"

"My brother and my uncle." When she didn't say anything for a minute, he asked, "Does that surprise you?"

She found herself frowning. "I didn't picture you as the family type."

He laughed. "And what type am I?"

Gorgeous. Scrumptious. Sophisticated. Refined. How did she put all that into words? She settled on, "A man who takes what he wants from life."

"And that rules out having a family?"

"In some cases it should."

"Is that what happened to you?" he asked, then hurriedly added, "Forget it. That's way too personal for a first date."

Harley smiled. "Is this a date?"

"Could be, though I have to admit I've never gone out with a woman whose name I don't know."

"It's Harley," she told him, rejecting Mona's suggestion of creating a new identity. She was who she was.

"Harley?" He sounded amused. "As in Davidson."

She laughed. "I was conceived on the road to the annual rally in Sturgis. My parents thought it appropriate."

"Your parents are bikers?"

Harley could almost imagine his smile. The thought gave her goose bumps. "Yes, but they finally grew up. They traded in the ape hangers for Gold Wings. Now they live on the road."

"No other family?"

"One sister."

"And her name is Honda?"

"Nope. Everly."

"As in Phil and Don?"

"You got it."

"Your parents weren't the born-to-be-wild type, huh?"

"From what I remember, they were more dazed and confused. But Everly and I turned out okay."

He took a long time to consider what she'd said. "Do you live alone?"

"Completely," she reassured the both of them.

"Good. Real good," he added.

And Harley felt a yearning like she'd never felt before.

"So, Harley with the wheat-field hair and bluebonnet eyes, where do we go from here?"

The yearning deepened. She licked her lips. "That depends on what you want."

The sound that rolled from his throat was a growl of hunger and nothing less. "I want *you*, Harley. I want the tension, the anticipation. I want to know you, inside out." He paused. "But I'm not that shallow. I can wait."

She couldn't breathe. Oh, God, she couldn't breathe. "Harley?"

With a shaking hand, she shifted the receiver to her other ear—the one that wasn't on fire. "I gu—" she started, then coughed and caught her air. "I guess that's as good a way as any to start a relationship."

"Is that what this is? A relationship?"

"No," she said firmly. "It's a date."

His chuckle rolled through her. "Then tell me, Harley. What do you do on a date?"

She groaned and remembered the Japanese film festival, the stock car finals, the batting cages. "Believe me, you don't want to know."

"You don't enjoy dating?"

"I don't have anything against the ritual. I just haven't had great luck in companions. I never quite understand their idea of fun. Or their conversations."

"Then there's no one special?"

"The last guy I went out with just left for Tibet."

"Tibet?"

"Never mind. It's a long story."

"Then, scratch it. I'd rather know what you like to talk about."

She wound the phone cord around her index finger. "I don't know. Anything. Simple things. Ask me a question."

"A question." He thought a moment. "Easy enough. What do you want for Christmas?"

"Christmas." Harley sighed. "I'm a kid when it comes to the holidays. I love the tinsel and ornaments, the lights, the cookies and candies." She moaned in delight. "And the fudge. Every year on Christmas Eve I make five pounds—all for me."

"And then you sneak downstairs before morning to check out what Santa left under the tree."

Harley laughed. "He'd have a pretty hard time at my place. My tree is sixty years old, fifteen inches high and ceramic, sprinkled with crystal lights and miniature candles. And since I never know where my parents will be, and Everly's rarely in town, I spend Christmas with friends, eat steamed turkey with sprout-and-tofu stuffing and exchange hideously ridiculous gag gifts."

Silence met her answer. Not a good sign. Maybe he was more traditional than his appearance led her to believe. What other conclusions might she have wrongly jumped to?

And what kind of misconceptions had he drawn about her?

"Have your Christmases always been so...original?" he finally asked.

"Maybe not original, but definitely fun." *Even if Everly and I did create the magic alone.* "I had a great time as a kid, sitting on Santa's lap and frosting cutout cookies and making ornaments out of salt dough. Everly and I took turns each year crowning the tree with the angel. Even during college I always made sure I was home to decorate the tree and stuff stockings."

"So what happened?"

Harley gripped the phone tighter and drew her knees to her chest. "I took a chance I shouldn't have."

"And you're afraid to do it again?"

She nodded, then softly whispered, "Yes."

Seconds passed and turned to minutes and Harley's heart counted every one.

"You still haven't answered my question."

"What question?"

"What do you want for Christmas?"

"I never ask for anything because it makes the surprises that much better. Everly always sends something she knows I'll never buy for myself. Like designer scents, cashmere or angora, satin sheets, lacy silk camisoles and tap . . . pants."

Harley let her voice trail off, hearing what she thought was a strangled whistle of breath. Then he cleared his throat.

"What do your parents give you?"

"Last year they sent me an iron bed frame they'd found in a barn in Kentucky. The headboard has the greatest scrollwork. After sandblasting away seventy-five years of Kentucky coal dust, I had it painted white." Harley ran her palm caressingly over her bed covering. "The year before they sent me an Appalachian wedding ring quilt. It looks like a bridal bed from a century ago. I love it."

"Are you in bed now?"

Uh-oh.

"Harley?"

"Yes," she answered slowly, touching her tongue to her upper lip.

"Tell me about your sheets."

Dangerous territory for a first conversation. "They're pink. Flannel. And soft. Like cotton balls. Or a kitten."

"Now tell me what you're wearing." His voice had grown deeper, yet his words were hushed, almost a whisper. And though his question was innocent, his intent was not.

She remembered his eyes, the sultry sweep of his lashes, the sleepy haze of dreams, and wondered how he'd look in bed beside her. Arousal spread through her without remorse.

She lifted the sheet and glanced at her nightgown. She'd chosen the one she wore with him in mind, knowing she was going to call, and wanting for some perverse reason to feel sexy when she heard his voice. This was *her* fantasy, after all.

"Harley, tell me."

She blew out a slow breath. "A nightgown, in an abstract pattern of deep pink, teal and peacock blue. It's silk, cut in a low scoop with thin straps. It laces down the back."

"All the way down the back?"

Her heart was thunder, a roller coaster, the roar of a jet plane. She swallowed hard. "To the top of . . . to the base of . . . to there."

"Tell me what it feels like."

Eyes closed, her senses took over. "When I walk, it floats around my ankles and slides against my thighs."

"And how does it feel in bed?"

"It's sleek. And cool. A caress on my skin." She was talking a hundred miles an hour now, wanting to get this over with, wanting to know what he wanted, why he wanted it from her.

And more than anything, why in the hell she wanted him.

"What else?"

"What else what?" she asked calmly, though her instincts said scream.

"What else are you wearing?"

Her nipples beaded. Her thighs grew warm. "Nothing."

"Not even one of those designer scents behind your knees?"

She inhaled as if by instinct, or his instruction. "It smells like clover, or honey and wildflowers. It's sweet, but not sticky. It reminds me of sunshine."

"Do you sleep on your back? On your side?" he asked, his voice pure gravel now.

Enough was enough. She swallowed hard, sweat building furiously at her nape. "Why do you want to know?"

This time his breathing was raw and ragged with need. "I want to climb up beside you. Feel your silk. Smell your sunshine. Taste your clover. I want to unlace your nightgown and pull you hard beneath me, until beginnings and endings and chances don't matter."

Harley pulled her nightgown to her toes, placed a pillow over her breasts. "You frighten me, Gardner."

"Do I? Are you sure you don't frighten yourself?"

"I don't know," she breathed.

"It's animal attraction, Harley. Plain and simple."

"I'm not sure I'm ready."

"Then sleep on it. Call me tomorrow. Or the day after. But call me. Call me."

The line went dead in her ear. Setting the phone on her dresser, she reached up and flipped off her lamp, leaving the lower light burning in the pedestal base. She needed that tiny bit of security as the emotions spinning through her threatened to whirl her into another dimension.

She curled tighter into her pillow, pressing her legs together. Her body burned. The soft silk chafed her nipples. And her belly quivered with the need to be filled.

Oh, God, why had she called? Why had she called? Her life had been so safe, so steady, so...antique. She'd been divorced for four years, her marriage a blur in her memory. But the slightest hint of male interest always brought to mind those years with Brad.

She couldn't call Gardner again, not after this, not after he'd flipped her world like a snowflake globe, leaving the pieces of who she had been to scatter at her feet. He raised too many questions, made her wonder if she'd been hiding. Made her wonder what she wanted.

No. That wasn't true. She knew exactly what she wanted. The same things so many wanted. Success. Happiness. Security. Love. Golden's Touch provided her with an incredible sense of fulfillment. Her strangely quixotic circle of friends were dearer to her than family.

And if she'd been hiding from anything, it was the fact that her drive for stability in life precluded having children.

She would never subject a child to her harried lifestyle. To the anxiety of last-minute travel plans, the days out of town that stretched into weeks. To her short bursts of temper brought on by the internal stress of wondering if a purchase would meet a client's needs, or if a buying trip had been a waste of time.

Children deserved better than emotionally exhausted and physically absent parents.

Or parents too absorbed in each other to remember they'd brought children into the world.

"YOU LOOK LIKE warm mash, boy."

Gardner set a stack of pancakes in front of his uncle, then started in on a batch for Ty. "Didn't get any sleep last night."

"You didn't say much when you got in from Houston last evening. I figured you still had money business on your mind," Judson said, drowning the pancakes in maple syrup.

If only his meandering attention could be explained away so easily, Gardner thought. "The meetings went good. The travel went bad. I had to leave the Cessna in San Antonio for service and catch a commercial flight to Dallas, then to Houston, then back to San Antonio. I had a lousy flight home."

"The Cessna still not running right?"

Gardner smiled wryly. "No. Pilot exhaustion."

Judson sliced through the stack with the side of his fork. "Understandable considering you covered half of Texas in one day."

Gardner poured a circle of batter onto the griddle. "Yeah, well, remind me to pick a smaller state next time I start up a ranch this size."

Judson chuckled. "Only problem with that is there ain't a hell of a lot of states a ranch this size would fit in."

"And this time next week Camelot will be twenty-five hundred acres bigger."

"Hmmm. Too bad it's going to waste," Judson said around a mouthful of pancakes.

"What do you mean going to waste?"

"Well, I'll be kickin' off here in a couple of years, and the way you're working you won't be far behind." Judson gestured with his fork. "You ain't doing much that I can see in the way of producing an heir."

"The only kicking I'm gonna do is hard across your butt if you don't mind your own business when it comes to my heirs."

"I call 'em like I see 'em, Gardner." Judson forked up another bite. "Tyler's got the right idea. Head up to Austin. Grab you a coed."

"You and Ty in this conspiracy together?"

Yawning, Tyler stepped off the bottom stair into the kitchen. Rubbing his eyes, he scraped back a chair from under the table and plopped down. "What conspiracy?"

Judson elbowed him in the ribs. "I was just telling your brother here that if he don't get himself a couple of kids, you're gonna be the owner of Camelot in a few years the way you're running around here breeding."

Ty blushed to the roots of his hair. "I'm not running around breeding. And if there's any conspiracy here it's you two butting into my sex life."

"Probably because you're the only one out of the three of us that has one," Gardner grumbled.

"Hey, the studies are true. A man at eighteen's in his prime." Beaming, Tyler cocked back his chair.

Judson snorted. "A man at eighteen's still a boy."

Gardner flipped Tyler's last pancake, served his brother, then started in on a batch for himself. "I don't know, Jud. Ty's been doing a man-size job for the past four years. I think he's earned the title."

"Thank you, big brother."

"As a matter of fact, Ty, I've got a man-size job for you when you get home from school. Sam Coltrain wants to lease the south sixty to run a few head. I need you to check the fence running over Little Creek." Gardner slapped butter on his pancakes. "Think you can handle that, big man?"

Ty's chewing slowed. "About after school, Gardner."

"Yeah?"

"I've got a major test in chemistry next week. I really gotta hit the books."

"Fine. Riding the fence line shouldn't take more than an hour or two."

"I was thinking of heading over to Tamara Shotweiler's house right after school. To study."

"You were thinking that, were you?" Gardner arched one brow. "You and who else?"

Tyler talked down to his plate. "Me and Tamara, Eric, Justin, Cory and Lynette."

"Sounds like a breeding party to me," Judson said, pushing away from the table and carrying his plate to the sink.

Gardner watched conflicting emotions flicker over Ty's face. There was no doubt his brother did a man's job, and his loyalty to the family business would win out every time over a pleasurable afternoon spent with friends—and one special girl.

But Gardner hated making Ty choose. He didn't feel he had the right to deprive his brother of his last months of high school fun. Come next fall, school would be all business. Tyler's dream to become a veterinarian wouldn't be sidelined by any number of coeds. Gardner knew his brother that well.

"What are you staring at?" Tyler snarled.

"You." Gardner smiled. "I'm jealous as hell."

"Of me?"

"I remember eighteen."

"Damn, Gardner. Your memory must be really good."

Gardner threw a pancake at his brother's head. "Funny, Tyler. Very funny. You go study. I'll check the fence across the creek. Right after I get back from talking to the drilling crew out in Acre 52."

Judson mashed his hat down to his ears and headed toward the back door. "You want me to have Ol' Pete fix up a bedroll for you?"

"No. I don't want to be out overnight. I'll take the Range Rover."

Both Tyler and Judson turned to stare. Gardner glared back. "What? A man can't sleep in his own bed if he wants to?"

"You ain't never cared where you slept, Gardner Barnes," Judson answered.

Tyler crossed his arms over his chest and leaned back in his chair. "Maybe he wants to get home because he's expecting another one of those late-night phone calls."

Gardner's spatula clattered against the stovetop. "What are you talking about?"

"I was minding my own business, drinking a glass of milk in my own kitchen." Tyler got up and walked through the motions. "The phone rang, so I picked it up like you told me."

"And you eavesdropped on a private conversation?"

"Nope. All I heard was you saying, 'I was wondering if you'd call.' Then she said—" Ty batted his lashes, laced his fingers beneath his chin "—'I was wondering myself.'"

Gardner popped his brother on the leg with a dish towel, but couldn't stop the smile pulling at his lips. "You go to school. And you—" he pointed at Judson "—see about that tractor."

"No need telling me what to do. I've been keeping Camelot's motors running since before you was born." Judson pushed open the screen door, then turned back. "Hey, Tyler. If the phone rings tonight, I'll get it. I need a cheap thrill."

Gardner glared. "If the phone rings tonight, neither one of you will get it."

Tyler headed upstairs, Judson out the door, both leaving their laughter bouncing off the walls of the kitchen. Gardner poured more batter, finishing off his pancakes while he cooked up breakfast for the rest of the men.

He had a decision to make. After hanging up last night before Harley could, he'd stayed in bed until dawn, imagining the classic lines of her body in a nightgown held up by strings. He'd thought of her beside him smelling like sunshine, and beneath him, her honey and clover his to take.

She appealed to him in so many ways, and at levels he was just now able to understand. Jud was right about Gardner's need to settle down, to start a family, to still the restlessness stirring in his blood. It didn't have anything to do with love.

So how far could he go without scaring Harley off? He couldn't believe some of the things that had come out of his mouth last night. But he'd been propped up in bed, naked, the sheet across his lap doing nothing to hide the effect she had on his libido.

And he'd wanted her to know up front about the primitive urges she roused in him. The feelings weren't new, only the intensity. She was nothing like what he'd thought she'd be.

Gardner grinned to himself, sliding a spatula beneath the last pancake. Cutout cookies and fudge. She didn't look the type. But he liked that about her. He liked it damn good. He wondered how many surprises she had in store for him. Because he intended to find out.

Oh, yes, he definitely intended to find out.

3

HARLEY TRIED the front door of Golden's Touch and found it locked. So far, so good. She'd spent the entire day shopping in Old Town Spring, hoping to avoid Mona and her questions. It looked as if her plan had worked. Slipping her key in the knob, Harley stepped inside.

No such luck. Mona stood in the center of the shop, her angled black hair framing her face, a pencil-thin Oriental sheath falling in a line of turquoise from her shoulders to mid-calf. Platform shoes gave her three inches of height advantage and she held her hands laced at her waist, meditation-style.

Harley closed the door. "Are you waiting for someone to make an offer?"

Mona's nose went up a notch. "I am unaffordable."

Briefly, Harley wondered if Gardner could afford her, then she clicked her tongue. "I pity poor Gibson."

"I never make Gibson pay."

"Then who bought the wine and candles and shrimp for the Florentine?" Harley asked, brushing by as she headed to her desk.

"Gibson was exhausted so he ordered in."

Harley glanced back over her shoulder. "Who did you find to deliver seafood?"

"We didn't have seafood. We ordered a—" Mona hesitated "—a pizza."

"You? A pizza? I'm surprised you're not in bed with a caloric hangover."

Mona pressed a hand to her stomach. "It was strictly vegetarian with an organic wheat crust and feta cheese, but I'm still feeling rather bloated today."

"Then go home. Put your feet up. Have a couple of sprouts for dinner." Harley pulled her organizer from her briefcase, flipped to the To Do section, then removed her ledger from the desk drawer. "I've got about five hundred things I need to finish up this afternoon. And if you don't leave, you're liable to find a price tag hanging from your earlobe."

"I hope that means you didn't get any sleep last night."

"I slept," she answered, dropping into her desk chair.

"Then you didn't call?"

Harley didn't even have to answer. Her heated face spoke for her.

"A-ha! You did." Mona perched her bottom on the edge of the desk. "I want to know every detail."

"There are no details."

"Start with what he sounds like."

"Is this the third degree?" Harley asked, realizing she'd forgotten—purposefully?—to tell Mona she'd heard Gardner's voice on the plane.

Mona scowled.

"All right. All right. His voice is deep, sexy, hypnotic." As deep and sexy and hypnotic as she'd expected. Even her body remembered. "He'd be the perfect host for a late-night radio show."

"Like Larry King?"

"No. Like the deejays who dedicate love songs to lonely hearts during the hours most sensible people are in bed."

"Hmmm. You stay up and listen to a lot of those, do you?"

"The only ones I've ever heard have been on TV. Or in books."

"How can you hear something in a book?"

"If you'd take the time to read one, you might just find out."

Mona glared. "Just tell me what he said."

I want to taste your clover. To pull you hard beneath me. Harley picked up her pencil. "He lives with his brother and his uncle."

"Where?"

"I'm not sure."

Mona slapped her palm on the open page of Harley's ledger. "You didn't ask?"

"His area code gives me a general idea."

"His area code covers half of West Texas, Harley. What does he do?"

"I don't know." Harley lifted Mona's hand away and turned to Dr. Fischer's account.

"You didn't ask that, either?"

"No."

"Why not?"

"I don't want to know where he lives or what he does." Harley tapped the eraser end of her pencil against her upper lip. "Gardner Barnes is so perfect, Mona. I'm not ready to put an end to the fantasy. Not yet."

Mona pressed her lips together. "You're afraid he'll turn out to be just like Brad."

"I can't help it. I spent four years married to a self-absorbed jerk who was God's physical gift to women." Twirling the pencil between two fingers, Harley grimaced at the pang of memory. "Lord knows he certainly let enough of them unwrap him."

"Brad had the mentality of a slug, Harley." Mona crossed her knees, the side slit of her dress revealing one slim leg. "I have to admit, though, if I was in need of a personal trainer I'd go for one with his bod. He obviously knows his stuff."

"Which is exactly why he did what he did. Brad needed constant admiration, from his co-workers, his clients. Even from me." *And fool that I was, I gave it to him and called it love.* Harley snorted. "Brad's entire self-worth is tied up in his biceps and quads and that muscle between his legs."

Mona assumed a look of extreme concentration. "I've always wondered if weight training develops every muscle a man has."

"Hmph. Women panted after him like rabid dogs. And he ate it up." Harley slumped back in her chair and tightened her grip on the pencil.

Mona blew out a puff of breath. "Men can be so shallow."

I want the tension, the anticipation. I want to know you, inside out. But I'm not that shallow. I can wait. Harley's pencil snapped. "Yeah, and I don't want to find out that Gardner Barnes is just as bad."

"So ask him what he does. Find out if he's all brawn and no brains."

"I can't. Not yet."

"That sounds like shallow judgment on your part."

"Maybe so, but it's my fantasy, all right? When I get to know him better, then I'll ask," Harley snapped, defensive, wondering when she'd decided she wanted to know him better.

Mona pursed her lips. "So all you found out was that he lives with his brother and his uncle? What did you talk about?"

"Mostly me." When Mona glared, Harley gave up and shoved the ledger away. "I don't know, Mona. He kept twisting the conversation, asking me questions."

"Is he going to call you?"

"I didn't give him my number."

Mona rolled her eyes. "Then you're going to call him back?"

"I might."

"You have to. At least to find out about the Excalibur's King thing."

"I don't know what to do." *Call me tomorrow. Or the day after. But call me. Call me.*

"Then give me the card." Mona held out her hand. "I'll call him."

"I can't. I burned it," Harley lied.

"What?" Mona shrieked.

"C'mon, Mona. What's the point? I'm obviously not who or what he thought I was."

"What makes you say that?"

"There were a lot of long silences in the conversation." Harley grimaced. "Usually right after I'd tripped over my tongue to give him the intimate details of my life."

"So you told him the truth about who you are?"

"I'm not going to lie about who I am. A man likes me or he doesn't."

Mona crossed her arms and gave Harley her best will-you-get-over-it glower. "Back to Brad, are we?"

Harley groaned and buried her face in her hands. "No. We're not back to Brad, we're back to me and what I want."

"And right now you *vant to be alone*."

"Only because I've got a lot of work to do and I don't want to be down here until midnight."

"Oh. Fine. I'll go," Mona said, miffed. "I don't need this abuse. I get enough of it from Gibson."

"Trouble in paradise?"

"He's having a mid-life crisis."

"Who? Mr. Show-Me-the-Way-To-the-Nearest-Party?"

Mona appeared deep in thought for a moment, then said, "He wants to have a baby."

"You're kidding." One look at her friend's face changed Harley's mind. "You're not kidding. What are you going to do?"

"When? Before or after my nervous breakdown?"

"Oh, Mona," Harley said, and pulled her dear friend close.

After a long moment, Mona sat back. She lifted her regal nose and sniffed. "Don't let this get around, Harley Golden, but I really am traditional at heart. Without order there is chaos."

"Order?" Harley couldn't help herself. "As in, first comes love, then comes marriage, then comes Mona with a baby carriage?"

"I suppose that's your idea of humor?"

Harley grimaced. "Pretty bad, huh."

"Pretty doesn't have anything to do with it."

"I don't know. Gibson would have to be a pretty big moron to let you get away," Harley said, and Mona finally smiled.

Once Mona was gone, Harley threw herself into the book work she should've finished last night. Every time her mind drifted to Gardner, she reminded herself he'd already cost her too much in time and emotion, not to mention self-examination.

Then her mind would drift to Mona, and Harley would strengthen her resolve. She had no room for a strong-willed, demanding, controlling man in her life.

The afternoon passed in a working blur, and by the time she'd dusted, moved the collector Christmas ornaments to a display in the front window and packaged up a silver urn to have reworked, she'd only thought of Gardner five more times.

Once she'd climbed the stairs to her apartment above the shop, she wasn't in the mood to cook. What she wanted to do was take a shower and clear Gardner Barnes from her mind once and for all.

But once she'd dried off, and pulled on a ragged, faded University of Texas T-shirt, she knew she wouldn't be able to get Gardner out of her head until she had all her answers. And the only way to get answers was to ask questions.

She climbed into bed and picked up the phone.

GARDNER WALKED INTO the kitchen at five to ten and checked the message board next to the phone. Nothing. Either she hadn't called or she hadn't left one. Slapping a chunk of chicken-fried steak and a squirt of ketchup between two slices of bread, he bounded up the stairs, leaving creek silt on the polished wood. Jud would kill him in the morning.

Scowling at the unblinking answering machine on his nightstand, Gardner stripped and ate the last two bites of his sandwich in the shower. Jumping out, he toweled off, pulling on his drawers and a pair of jeans once he was half-dry.

No way was she catching him naked again.

And no way was he letting the talk get out of hand. Assuming she called. Which was assuming a lot, considering the direction he'd carried their conversation last night.

It wasn't the devil that made him do it, but the sound of Harley's voice. And the mental image her words painted on the blank canvas of his mind. He'd never been so turned on while in a room alone.

He had no problem giving Harley time and space to figure out how fast and how far she wanted to take this thing. But he had no idea how to find her. And that bothered him more than he cared to admit. Because last night might have started out as a date, but it ended up involvement.

As involved as he'd been in a very long time.

He was on his sixth barefoot trip across the bedroom's expanse of hunter green carpet when the phone rang. He took a deep breath, flexed his fingers and swore he was going to pull the jack from the wall if this was a wrong number.

"Hello?"

"This time I ask the questions."

Gardner released his breath in a long, slow stream. "Anything you want."

After several seconds, she chuckled softly. "Are you always so agreeable?"

"Ask my brother or my uncle and you'll get a definite no. But I've been looking forward to this all day." He relaxed enough to sit on the edge of the bed. "I'm in the mood for whatever you want."

"Tough day at the office, huh?"

"A long one, anyway," Gardner answered, rolling his shoulders to relieve the effects of driving from Acre 52 to Little Creek in one day. "And half of it spent behind a steering wheel. I just pulled in thirty minutes ago."

"Do you travel a lot?"

"Only when I can't get out of it. I don't like to be away from home more than I have to."

"Because of your brother and uncle?"

"That, plus the responsibilities involved in being the boss. Thank God I've only got a crew of eight to manage."

She was quiet for a minute, as if digesting that bit of information. "Your brother and your uncle, are they your only family?"

"Yeah." Feet flat on the floor, Gardner lay back on the bed. "My mother died of cancer, my father of grief six months later, both when I was twenty-two."

"I'm sorry."

Her simple words prompted him to say more. "Tyler, my brother, he was only ten. It was tough, watching my mother suffer. But it was almost worse the morning my father didn't get out of bed."

He didn't tell her about the note. Or the tranquilizers. Or the decision he'd made that day. He would never love with the fierce intensity that drove a man to his father's madness.

Never.

He stared at the circle of light the lamp cast onto the ceiling. "If it hadn't been for Judson, my uncle, I might've lost Ty. But my father had named Judson Ty's guardian and left everything he owned to the three of us."

"You must be proud of the home you've made for them."

"They're my family. How could I do anything else?"

"It's been known to happen."

"Yeah, well, not with the Barneses. Tyler being so young and all when it happened, I sometimes forget I'm not his father." Gardner scratched his bare chest, then stopped scratching when Harley chuckled.

"If he hasn't left home yet, you must be doing something right."

"He's a good kid. But the real test will come next fall. He's headed to Texas A & M."

"Following in big brother's footsteps?"

"His aspirations are a little bit higher. He's got his heart set on becoming a veterinarian."

Harley whistled. "That'll cost a pretty penny."

"He's worth it." Gardner plumped up two green-and-russet throw pillows and leaned against the old headboard. "What else do you want to know?"

"Have you ever been married?"

He laughed. "No."

"Why is that funny?"

"It's not the idea of marriage that's funny. I was just wondering if we'd get around to the personal stuff on our second date or wait till the third."

She paused, as if feeling her way, then took a deep breath and plunged in. "The way we ended last night, I didn't think there was anything too personal to discuss."

Oh, he could get a hell of a lot more personal, but he wasn't going to frighten her off by telling her that. "No, I've never been married."

"And how many conquests have you made with the business-card routine?"

"I'm working on my first." When she didn't answer he added, "Believe it or don't, but I never lie."

"You managed the technique so smoothly I assumed you'd had years of practice."

"I didn't even think of it until the plane touched down. Sorry if I embarrassed you."

"Don't be. Like I said, I figured you for a man who takes what he wants from life."

Gardner switched off the bedside lamp, plunging the room into intimate darkness. The shadows made his confession easier. "Two days ago I thought I had all life could offer. There was nothing I needed to take. And then I saw you."

"And what, Gardner? What made me different?"

He sensed the frustration in her voice. It nearly equaled his own. But he couldn't put into words what he'd seen in her. All he knew was that she touched him. He wanted to touch her back.

"Gardner?" Harley prompted.

"I don't know, Harley. I looked up and there you were. Beautiful. Elegant. I felt . . . Hell, I don't even know what I felt."

"What you saw, Gardner . . ." Harley hesitated, her voice growing frantic, insistent. "That wasn't me. The suit. The heels. That's not who I am."

"You're talking about looks, Harley." Gardner got to his feet, the full moon shining through the window above his bed. "And what you told me last night showed me more."

"I don't remember telling you much. And what I do remember is so boring."

Gardner chuckled. "If that was boring, I don't think I could survive your idea of fun."

"I'm not talking about . . . that."

"You mean what you wear to bed?" He smiled at her groan. "That's only part of it, Harley. And, yes, I spent a lot of time today picturing you in that gown." And in a helluva lot less, he silently added. "But I also remember the excitement in your voice when you talked about Christmas, and about being a kid."

She gave a tiny laugh. "Amazing how first impressions can be so distorted."

Gardner crossed his room, propped his hip against the corner of his dresser. "I like second ones better."

"So do I, though I have to plead guilty to judging you by your looks."

"And what did *you* see?" He glanced over his shoulder to the mirror behind him.

"Success. I had no trouble picturing your face on the cover of *CFO* or *Forbes*. Or even *GQ*."

Try *Western Horseman*, Gardner mused, studying the crow's-feet the sun had carved into his skin. "Is that good or bad?"

"Neither and both. It made it hard to call the first time, and even harder to call today."

Gardner frowned. "Why?"

She gave a self-conscious little laugh. "I've run into too many men who use their looks to get what they want in their professional lives. Not to mention their personal lives."

Old wounds, Gardner reflected. Interesting. "That works both ways, you know."

"Touché. Maybe I'm oversensitive."

Maybe she had reason to be. "Believe me, looks don't matter in my business. And as far as my personal life, well, I've been too busy with business to have one."

He thought of the heirs he didn't have and resumed pacing. "For the past couple of days, though, I haven't been able to get you out of my mind long enough to concentrate on what has needed to be done."

"I've been a little preoccupied myself."

"Then what are we going to do about it?" He stopped
at the foot of his bed and closed his eyes. Leaning his
head back, he swallowed the lump of longing in his
throat. "Tell me where you are. I'll be there tomorrow."

"On a moment's notice? What about business?"

"Screw it. The crew can handle moving the—"

"Wait. Stop."

He switched the receiver to the other ear. "Why?"

"Don't tell me what you do. This is *my* fantasy. I want
to know the Gardner Barnes you don't share with anyone else."

Fantasy, huh? Gardner shoved his fingers over his
hair and blew out a breath. "That's asking a hell of a
lot."

"I know I'm complicating things. But I can't think of
a simple way to put what I'm feeling into words."

"Just spell it out."

"I need . . . I want . . . no, I *don't* want to jump into
anything without knowing what I'll find when I get
there. That's why I don't want to see you face-to-face.
You're too . . . distracting."

"Distracting?" Gardner rubbed the base of his neck.
"I've been called a lot of things, but I don't think that's
one of them."

"You can't be blind to your looks." She sounded incredulous.

"Like you said, what I look like doesn't have much
to do with anything."

"What *do* you look like?"

He frowned. "You know what I look like."

"No. I mean right now." She seemed to hesitate.
"Gardner?"

He loved it when she said his name in that breathy voice. "Hmmm?"

"What are you wearing?"

He laughed. Payback time. "That's a hell of a question to be asking a man at eleven o'clock at night, Harley."

He could almost feel her blush through the phone. "Well?"

A fearless woman. Outstanding. "Jeans."

"That's it?"

"And my Fruit of the Looms. And, yes," he continued before she could ask more. "They're all I sleep in."

"Then you're not in bed now?"

He swallowed a heady groan. "No, but I should be."

"So do you want to tell me what your bed looks like?"

This sharing of information was not going the way Gardner had planned. "It's an antique four-poster that belonged to my grandparents," he said, addressing the matter impersonally. "It's heavy, dark oak. The candlewick quilt is almost as old."

His throat grew tight. "But talking about beds is going to get us in trouble, Harley. Just like talking about your nightgown and the way I want to take it off.

"I picture you, Harley." Gardner curled his fingers into the paper-thin coverlet. "I see you stretched out on my bed. Telling me about the cookies you made. Feeding me a bite of fudge. I think how good you'd smell wearing chocolate. How much better you'd taste."

"Gardner—"

"No, wait." The same frustration that threaded his voice filled his jeans. He couldn't go on not knowing more.

"What?" she asked on a shaky sigh.

"Tell me your last name."

For a moment, he heard nothing but breathing, then she whispered, "Golden."

Gardner expelled a sigh of relief. Harley Golden. Perfect. His desperation eased.

"Well, Harley Golden. It's eleven o'clock. Saturday night is just beginning for you and your sprout-and-tofu friends." Gardner grimaced. When put that way, their differences sounded insurmountable.

"You've had a long day."

"And I'm in desperate need of a shower." He didn't bother to tell her he'd already had one. Or that he'd pictured her beside him standing under the spray. Or that he wanted her there with him now. "You wouldn't want to take one with me, would you?"

She sucked in a sharp breath. "I don't . . . I can't . . ."

Her voice trailed off and Gardner flexed his fingers around the phone. "I could use your help washing my back."

"I always have trouble—" she paused, then whispered "—you know . . . reaching between my shoulder blades."

"Yeah, that's the spot. How 'bout it, Harley? We could use your soap."

She never missed a beat. "I bet you'd smell good in clover, Gardner. I bet you'd . . ."

"What, Harley?" he rasped.

"I bet you'd taste even better."

Gardner released the button fly of his jeans.

"Wet skin is so sweet," Harley went on. "Like honey. Especially when the water's warm. As warm as sunshine."

Reaching down, he pressed against the ache growing heavier with Harley's every word.

"A shower's nice, but I've always wanted to bathe outdoors. In a cold stream, when the sun's beating down. Or at night."

Gardner dropped his head back and stroked his urgently building need. "Harley—"

"Imagine a cool breeze. And a warm, bubbling spring." Her voice dropped to a low murmur. "My skin tingles when I think about it. And when I picture you beside me, I grow—"

"Enough!" Gardner flipped on every light in the room. "Don't do this, Harley. Unless you're ready for me to find you."

"No. Not yet."

A strange relief left Gardner calm. He glanced down at his erection. Aroused, but calm. She was right. It was still too soon. There was more to compatibility than physical attraction, though right now fifty years of mindless sex sounded damn good.

"Same time tomorrow?"

"Unless Sunday's not good for you," Harley answered.

"Any time's good for me." But not as good as it's gonna get, Harley Golden. Nowhere near as good.

"I'll call tomorrow night."

"See that you do," he replied, then severed the connection and shucked off his jeans and his Fruit of the Looms, returning to the bathroom for a long, cold shower.

HARLEY REFOLDED THE PAPER, stacked it atop the others littering her kitchen table, then sat back in her chair. Propping her feet on the one beside her, she sipped her tea.

She'd spent the morning doing just as Mona predicted. And though it proved she was a predictable bore, the time had been well spent. An antique auction to be held Tuesday in Fredericksburg listed not only rare bottles but hospital supplies among its inventory. The sale had all the earmarks of the jackpot she needed to knock out her arrangement with Dr. Fischer.

The only problem was what to wear. Her business wardrobe worked well for the more formal estate and antique auctions she attended in the northeast, but suits and heels wouldn't do for an open-air barn in central Texas.

This called for extreme measures. A shopping trip to the Galleria. Structured sweaters, long skirts and boots ought to do the trick. And since it was close to noon she had to get moving. Lack of motivation wasn't a problem. Lack of energy was.

Even though she'd allowed herself the luxury of sleeping late, her rest had been fretful, filled with dreams of Gardner Barnes and showers and antique four-poster beds. Her own fault, really, though she had no explanation beyond insanity for the direction she'd steered their conversation. She blushed, remembering the picture of her words, and Gardner's strangled moans.

She wasn't a flirt, and she certainly wasn't a tease—with Brad's generous help, her marriage had suffered blows from women who were both. But something about Gardner Barnes made her want to test the bounds of propriety.

She'd wanted answers, explanations as to why she couldn't get him out of her mind. As Mona had so aptly put it, Harley Golden did not do gorgeous men. But when she listened to Gardner, she never thought of how he looked, only of his words, the way he loved his family, the kind of man he was.

The kind of man she'd always wanted.

Talking to Gardner brought it all back, dreams she hadn't considered for a very long time. And she didn't even remember forgetting them. Funny, when they'd been so important when she was a child.

She hadn't lied to Gardner. Not about her memories of Christmas. Or the fact that she and Everly had turned out okay. She just hadn't admitted that she and her sister owed their well-adjustment to each other more than to either of their parents. Buck and Trixie had provided the roof and the food. Anything more was a stretch of their parenting skills.

Harley had always hated Sunday mornings. By the time she knew to distinguish the first day of the week from the rest, she'd dreaded the long hours spent on the back of a Harley-Davidson behind her mother. She'd wanted to spend the mornings at Sunday school, then come home to platters of fried chicken, or pot roast and mashed potatoes.

Once she and Everly were old enough to stay home alone, Buck and Trixie had extended the hours of their Sunday rides, leaving Harley to wonder why they'd ever had children to begin with, seeing as they had no time to invest in raising them. The lack of nurturing from her parents had cemented her decision not to have children of her own.

Today was a perfect example of her sporadic schedule. Buying trips came up on the spur of the moment, without regard to the time of the year—or a child's needs. Harley remembered too well those times as a child when her parents weren't there when she needed them.

And it was her own conscience she had to live with, after all.

She sipped at her tea and fleetingly wondered how Gardner had spent his Sundays as a child, went on to wonder how he spent them now, wondered finally if a burst of melancholy was a good enough reason to call.

4

"IS THIS a bad time to call?"

Surprised to hear Harley's voice, Gardner took a moment to reply. "No. I mean, don't worry about it. Any time is good."

"I wasn't sure you'd be home."

Glancing down at his dusty jeans and sweat-soaked denim shirt, then at the baloney sandwich he held in one hand, Gardner wondered if destiny had driven him to hunger the exact moment Harley decided to call.

"Gardner?" She sounded unsure.

"I just stopped in to grab a bite to eat. Five minutes either side of this one, and you would've missed me."

"Then you're going back out. This *is* a bad time."

Gardner took a bite and slowly chewed. In addition to uncertainty, he sensed her need to talk. Serious talk, friend-to-friend talk.

And she'd chosen him.

Unwilling to disappoint her, or himself, he scraped back a kitchen chair and sat. "No. It's a good time. I've been up since before dawn. A break is exactly what I need right now."

"You don't take Sundays off?"

"Once in a while. I try to get into church with Judson and Ty at least a couple of times a month."

"But not today?"

"I couldn't make it." Judson didn't take kindly to his family falling asleep in the church pews, and staying on the move was the only thing keeping Gardner awake. After Harley's phone call and his second shower, he'd spent the hours until dawn on horseback.

This morning he was running on caffeine and pure determination. "I had a horse pull up lame last night. I tended to him until the doc could make it out this morning."

"You have horses?"

Gardner grinned privately. "A few."

"Polo ponies? Or jumpers?"

"I don't think I should answer that, Harley." Gardner tore off another chunk of sandwich and popped it into his mouth. "That would be telling more about me and my business than you said you wanted to know."

"You're probably right." After a lengthy silence, Harley sighed. "Can I ask you something else instead?"

"Sure," Gardner said and, with the remainder of his sandwich in hand, cocked his chair back to rest against the narrow strip of wall beside the refrigerator.

"How did you spend your Sundays as a child?"

He grinned to himself at the absurdity of her question. "Besides the two hours I fidgeted during church services waiting to get home and watch football?"

"A hard-core fan, huh? Did you play in school?"

"Nope. District enrollment was too small. My senior class could've fielded a six-man team as long as two of the men were women."

"You're kidding." Harley sounded incredulous. "That sounds awfully. . . rural."

"Rural. Isolated. You name it," he said, wondering if he heard distaste or disbelief in Harley's voice.

"So how many were in your graduating class?"

"Four guys and fourteen girls." Gardner laughed. "Some odds, huh?"

"Yeah, lucky you."

"The other three guys were even luckier."

"How so?" Harley asked.

"I was so intent on expanding the family business that I took myself out of competition."

"I'm not surprised."

"Why not?"

"That aura of success. Carrying it off as naturally as you do comes from wearing the look for a very long time."

Bringing his chair back down on four legs, Gardner leaned forward and frowned. "I'd be flattered if the truth wasn't quite so hard to live with these days."

"In what way?"

He thought of his nonexistent heirs again. And then he thought of Harley. Only Harley. "That single-minded focus has caused me to miss out on a lot of life. I've been wondering lately—" *the past couple of days of knowing you, to be exact* "—if it's too late to make up for what I've missed."

"What do you think you've missed?" Her question held a trace of a smile.

Gardner thought a moment, and reminisced on how he'd gotten where he was today. He'd seen his father bypass one business opportunity after another for the simple reason that he'd been unwilling to spend time away from home. Gardner had invested all of those hours—and more—researching mineral rights and oil leases, cattle breeds and insemination programs.

He'd studied outside his college courses, poring over agricultural markets and trends, determined to make the land pay, determined to make his father remember that, in addition to a wife, he had two sons.

Shaking off that disturbing thought, Gardner returned to Harley's question. "What I've missed out on most has to be relationships. I haven't kept in touch with any of my classmates from high school or college. And work has been my mistress for as many years as I can remember."

"Is that your version of safe sex?"

Gardner laughed. "I guess you could say that. Though I think I'm gonna have to give her up and settle down."

"Why's that?"

"She provides her own sort of satisfaction, but she doesn't have what it takes to carry on the family name." Leaning forward, Gardner reached into the fridge for a cola. He popped the top and sipped. "Ty's got a hell of a future waiting for him, and Jud's done the work of ten men in his lifetime.

"Neither one of them has the desire to continue what I've started. If I don't get busy and start thinking about a family, I'm not going to have anyone to leave this empire to."

"Do you think you'll be able to do that?"

He frowned. "Do what?"

"After a lifetime of working at the pace you have, will you be able to slow down enough to raise a family?"

He thought of his vow never to love and wondered if Harley had somehow picked up on it. "I've built a good, comfortable life. The time I invest in business now is more on upkeep or maintenance than expansion.

"I'd like to share my success before I get too old to enjoy it. And I'd like to know there's someone to leave it to after I'm gone."

"That's an interesting rationale for wanting a family."

Gardner chuckled. "I don't think there's anything wrong with the rationale. Maybe I just didn't state it as romantically as a woman would like. I mean, having a family is not something I plan to do on my own."

Feeling mired in a conversation that had grown too deep, Gardner ended with, "So how 'bout it, Golden? You wanna get hitched?"

Harley blew an inelegant snort right into his ear. "Forget it, Barnes. I've got better ways to spend my Sundays than watching football."

"Oh, yeah? Name one."

"Today I'm going shopping. You know how it is. So many stores, so little time."

He sipped his drink. "Now there's a great time if I ever heard one. Would I like what you're going to buy?"

"Probably not, which is a good thing, because I'm not getting into any more suggestive conversations with you."

"Can't take the heat, huh?"

"I can take anything you can dish out, mister. But right now I don't have the time. I've got a business trip to plan."

"When are you leaving?" he asked, not liking the news.

"Tomorrow. And unfortunately I don't have a thing to wear."

Which is exactly what he'd like to see her in. Not a thing. "Harley?"

"Hmmm?"

"Will you call me tonight?"

"That depends."

"On what?"

"If between now and then, I decide that talking to you is worth the long-distance phone bill I'm going to be getting next month."

"I'll call. Give me your number."

"Not yet."

"Then call me collect."

"I'll think about it."

"You do that. And trust me on this one, Harley Golden," Gardner demanded with a growl. "I'm the best investment you've ever made in your life."

"Think so, huh?"

Feeling his body heat rise, Gardner ran the cold drink can over his forehead. "Believe me, I'm worth your while."

"Braggart."

"I told you before, I never lie."

"Well, if I can scrape up the energy after a day of shopping, I'll call."

"Harley?"

"Hmmm?"

"One more thing."

"Just one," she said.

He pictured her holding up a single finger.

"And it can't involve beds, nightgowns or showers."

He shook his head, enjoying her humor and the fact that she could tease about a subject that had nearly gotten out of hand.

"Gardner, what is it?" she prompted when he remained silent.

"I was wondering if you got what you needed from this call."

"Yeah," she said, her voice that sexy sigh he loved to hear. "I think I did."

"Good. I'll talk to you this evening." Gardner rang off and sat in his kitchen. The silence of the house enclosed him in familiarity and comfort.

He had no reason not to believe that he'd fulfilled whatever need Harley had for calling. No reason at all, except the niggling concern that she was having second thoughts about him, about what they'd started, maybe even about herself.

He'd wager King's next six calves that somewhere in her life she'd had her confidence shattered. He wondered how, and by whom, then realized it didn't matter. He wasn't going to give up on her because of that.

But thinking about Harley and heirs in the same breath cemented his need to know more. Her parents were bikers. She ate tofu for Christmas. Her designer tastes required money. A lot of money. Not that he was one to jump to conclusions, but he was one to be safe rather than sorry.

He glanced at the cracked face of his watch. In a matter of minutes, Judson and Ty would be rolling in, which gave him just enough time to make a call.

He picked up the phone and dialed directory assistance. After jotting Harley's number on the tablet by the phone, he ripped the paper in half and stuffed the note in his pocket.

Then he made a second call to a number he knew by heart. A number that belonged to a person who provided him facts and figures and background information anytime—and on anyone—he needed.

HARLEY'S STRANGE TRIP into melancholy vanished by the time she returned from shopping. When had she ever made so many impulsive purchases in one single day? Mona and Everly would both be proud.

The long denim skirt and Navajo blanket wrap would be perfect to wear to the country auction with her riding boots and handkerchief-linen blouse. But what she absolutely couldn't wait to wear—and still couldn't believe she'd bought—was a pair of cherry red jeans and matching Justin ropers.

She hadn't owned a pair of jeans since... when? They'd certainly been BB—Before Brad. Obviously, her subliminal conscious had still been shopping with Brad's tastes in mind. Had she shopped today for herself, or for Gardner Barnes?

Call-waiting beeped on the line while she was making arrangements with a bed-and-breakfast near Fredericksburg.

"Do you need to get that?" asked the clerk. "I'll be glad to hold."

"No. If it's important, they'll call back," she answered, and finished making her reservations.

When the phone rang a second time a couple of hours later, she was struggling into her freshly washed and dried and shrunk-at-least-one-size red jeans. She belly flopped across the bed and jerked up the receiver.

"Hello?"

"Miss Golden? Dr. Fischer here."

She suppressed a groan, hoping he would ask if this was a good time so she could say no. "Dr. Fischer. What can I do for you?"

"I'm just following up on the message I left you Friday. Have you had an opportunity to pursue my lead?"

Give a girl a chance, will ya, Doc? "I'm afraid I didn't have any luck locating the bottle in Spring. None of the shop owners I spoke with remembered having stocked or sold one recently. I did find a pharmacist's scale, however."

"Wonderful. When can I see it?"

"It's being couriered over tomorrow, but I'm leaving first thing in the morning for central Texas. I won't be back in town before the end of the week." Harley didn't tell him about the bottles or the hospital supplies, for fear he'd hunt her down.

"I can't say I'm not disappointed, but perhaps you'll have more to show me when you return."

"There's a good chance," Harley assured him. "I've had phenomenal luck finding hidden treasures at small estate sales."

"You will be in touch, won't you?"

"Of course, Doctor."

"Until then. And, Miss Golden—"

"Yes?" she prompted.

He cleared his throat. "Thank you for your efforts. Re-creating the history of medicine has become an obsession with me. I appreciate your hard work."

"You're welcome, Dr. Fischer." Harley hung up feeling guilty for every uncharitable thought she'd had about the man.

After struggling out of the jeans, she folded them, having decided they would work better on a day for browsing through shops than on a day of driving. To drive, she needed to breathe.

She'd just pulled her overnighter from the closet when the phone rang again. Not wanting to chance another guilt trip with Dr. Fischer, she let the answering machine pick up.

I am currently unavailable, Harley mouthed along with the recording, then added verbally, and very loudly, "And I intend to be so for the next twelve hours."

The beep sounded and Harley waited. And waited. And had her hand halfway to the receiver when she heard, "Harley?"

Gardner. He'd found her. She didn't know whether to be thrilled or annoyed.

"Don't pick up if you're there."

As if she was about to give him the satisfaction? Uh-uh. Not a chance.

"I just wanted you to know that I'd looked you up. I don't want any secrets standing in the way. And I'm not going to show up unannounced. I could find you. But I think I'll let you come to me. I want you to call the shots. This is your fantasy, after all.

"So tell me what you want. Tell me what turns you on. Tell me your darkest secrets, your deepest desires. But be warned. Tonight I want you. Fiercely. And what I can't do to your body, I plan to do to your mind. Call me, when the waiting gets to be too much. Call me. Call—" *Beeeeeeeeep.*

The click and whir of the machine barely registered. All Harley heard was Gardner's voice. Lowering the volume completely, she rewound the tape, then took her phone off the hook, though she knew with a sixth sense of certainty that he wouldn't call again.

He'd told her what he wanted—and what he wanted from her. The question was whether or not Gardner Barnes was the man to meet her needs.

She had too much of the real stuff yet to learn. All those things that might spoil her fantasy. Would he leave beard stubble in the sink? Would he eat the last four Oreos she'd stashed away for a bout of PMS?

Would he cuddle her close after they made love or roll over and go to sleep?

Harley reconnected her phone. A smug smile pulled at her lips. Oh, she'd wait all right. She'd wait until she was sure Gardner couldn't stand it any more. Then she'd call and let him know just exactly who was in charge of this relationship.

He wanted fantasy? Easy. She was working on a doozy. He wanted secrets? Fine. She had ones she'd never told a living soul. He wanted desires? No problem. She'd give him a phone call to knock his socks off.

GARDNER HAD JUST come up with another name to call himself using the word *ass* when the phone rang. Fully clothed, he carried the portable phone outside—away from his bedroom and his bed. Easing down into the porch rocker, he answered.

"I didn't want you to find me," she said, sounding more playful than upset.

"I didn't find you, Harley. I found your phone number."

"My phone number tells you where I am."

"Your phone number puts you in one of the biggest urban sprawls in the country." He cringed at the thought that she could live like that. "I'm not coming to Houston to find you until you tell me to."

"You broke the rules. I think you need to be punished."

Punished? That sounded promising. "What kind of punishment did you have in mind?"

"*I'm* going to talk. *You're* going to listen."

Okay. She'd warned him. He could buck up and handle her idea of punishment. Studying the toes of his boots, he set the rocker in motion and forced himself to relax. "I'm all ears."

"I thought about you earlier," she began. "When I was in the shower. I never realized how many hard-to-reach spots there are on the female body."

"Besides your back?"

"I told you to listen," she admonished. "If you don't behave, I'll have to stop your punishment."

He took an immediate vow of silence.

"That's better. Now, I thought I'd let you know that the back of my thighs is another place I have trouble getting to. I feel like I'm doing a contortionist act, you know, twisting and bending. If you'd been there, it would have been much easier."

No. It would have been much harder.

"But we've already talked about baths and showers. And beds. Though I did change my sheets tonight with you in mind. I wasn't sure what kind of sheets go with Fruit of the Looms. I started digging in the linen closet and found a perfect pair. Everly sent them to me last year on my birthday."

Sweat broke out on Gardner's brow. He dropped his hat to the porch beside him and buried his face in the crook of his denim-covered elbow.

"They're satin. Hot pink drizzled in black."

Gardner stretched out his legs and groaned. He'd be fine. He really would.

"I thought about wearing a gown. But then I thought of you."

Gardner popped the snaps down the front of his shirt and leaned back in the rocker, the mound of his zipper pointing straight to the moon.

"I have on panties, if you can call them that. They cover most of what they're supposed to. The lace cups of the bra don't cover anything. But I think that's the whole point. Don't you?"

Oh, yeah. He got the point. And the point was getting harder.

"Oh," she went on, Miss Innocent if there ever was one. "Did I tell you they're black? Except for the garter belt. It's the same color as the sheets. And the stockings are fishnet.

"I lit a few candles when I got into bed, you know, thinking of you. The room smells honey sweet," she murmured appreciatively. "I left the rest of the lights off so the shadows on the wall flicker.

"I wasn't sure what to do with my hair so I piled it on top of my head. I'll let you take it down. Is that okay?"

"Hmmm?" he replied.

"I even put on lipstick." She moaned as if running her tongue over her lips. "I thought it might be fun to leave marks on your body. Everywhere I kiss you. And, Gardner?"

"Huh?" he barely managed to respond.

"I plan to kiss you everywhere." She kissed into the phone. "Sweet dreams."

Gardner hung up once he realized the buzzing in his head was the dial tone. Shoving off his shirt, he stood, jerked his boots and socks from his feet and walked barefoot across the yard. Dazed, he dropped his jeans and drawers inside the corral and went face first into the horse trough.

"You feelin' okay, boy?"

Gardner stared blankly at his uncle, then at the pile of scrambled eggs and hot buttered toast steaming on the table. "What makes you ask?"

"Oh, little things. Like the clothes I found scattered across the yard this morning. I thought in a fit of delirious fever you mistook the horse trough for your bathtub."

Judson turned from the stove. "But now that you're standing here dripping on my floor, wearing nothing but a towel, I'm thinking maybe your fever's in your brain."

"Sorry," Gardner mumbled. "I showered in the bunkhouse. I didn't have a change of clothes—" he glanced down "—or a bigger towel." After his dunking in the trough, he couldn't handle the prospect of sleeping alone in his own bed, so he'd bedded down on a pallet of saddle blankets in the barn.

Last night he'd figured discomfort was the way to go. The spring-fed waters that pumped into the bunkhouse well had done a good job cooling his physical fever. But standing here, looking like a loon dripping onto Judson's clean floor, brought it all back.

Once he got through with her, Harley Golden wouldn't know the meaning of punishment. He planned to turn her inside out.

"Gardner!"

His head snapped up.

"Grab the mop out of the laundry room and clean up this mess," Judson ordered, gesturing with one hand while he scrambled more eggs with the other. "And you might give a wipe to the stairs, too, considering it's your dirt still sittin' there, and dammit, boy, fasten that towel tighter. This ain't no porn show."

Water dripped down Gardner's back and into the towel knotted at his waist. He bit off a curse and spun around, grabbing the mop from the corner behind the washing machine. He soaked up the puddle and swiped his way up the stairs.

A yawning Ty waited for him at the top. "You forget where your bathroom is, big brother?"

Gardner brandished the mop head like a weapon. Ty jumped back. "Last time I looked it was two doors down the hall from yours. You got a problem with that, I'll lend you my suitcase."

"Why would I want to go anywhere? I've got a front-row seat to the Gardner Barnes Show. Or is it—" Ty hid half his face with one hand "—the Phantom of the Ranch? He wears his towel to hide his shame."

"I'll show you shame," Gardner growled. The mop clattered to the floor. He whipped off his towel and, with a flick of his wrist, wound it into a twisted rope. Before Ty could think to blink, he found himself calf-tied, one ankle and two wrists bound together. "Let's see you get yourself out of that one, college boy."

Ty worked at the knot. "At least I'm not the one standing naked in the hall."

"Tyler, that you I hear up there?"

"Be right down, Uncle Jud," he called, then grumbled to himself, "Soon as I figure out how to scoot bass-ackward down the stairs."

"Ty," Judson called again. "If your brother's still standing there, tell him he left the damn phone outside last night. I got his boots and hat off the porch, but he's gonna have to get the rest of his clothes out of the corral hisself."

Tyler lay back on the wooden floor and grinned. "More late-night phone calls, big brother?"

Gardner scowled down. "What we ought to be talking about here is not my phone calls, but the Friday-afternoon excuse of studying you used to get out of

chores, and the fact that you didn't make it home with
a single book. Leave them over at Tamara Shotweiler's, did you?"

Ty colored, then smiled as inspiration struck. "I don't
know, Gardner. I'm thinking maybe what we ought to
talk about is me laying here tied up and you standing
there butt-naked."

Gardner jerked the towel free from Ty's arms. "Get
downstairs to breakfast and see to it that you're here
after school." He knotted the towel at his waist. "And
as far as studying goes, just make me proud, Tyler."

Gardner slammed the door to his bedroom on the
sound of his brother lumbering down the stairs.
Knowing he deserved every bit of ribbing he got from
both Ty and Jud didn't make it easier to swallow the fact
that he was being led around by his libido like it was
filling in for his brain.

He knew why Harley had done what she'd done. If
their relationship held to convention, last night
would've been their third date. Harley had decided to
show him her strength, to tell him she was an equal
partner with equal say. She'd taken charge and, instead of a kiss to get the juices of imagination stirring,
she'd given great talk.

Gardner had been stirred by her words and her feminine power, stirred enough to want to take this relationship further. He didn't mean to bed, not right now,
though he knew they were headed there eventually.

He could do worse for himself than a woman with
Harley's imagination. Sexual compatibility went a long
way in a marriage—especially a loveless marriage.

If he'd never seen her, he'd be more content to let
things ride. But knowing what she looked like, more

than liking what he saw and the awareness that she felt the same put a twist to the tension of the phone calls.

Gardner didn't know which was twisted more, his mind or his gut. The hard-on he could live with, or at least work around. But the mind games made for bad business.

He figured he could afford to take a couple of days off—more like, he couldn't afford not to. Judson was right. He had a fever. He needed a cure in a bad way.

If she called tonight, he'd find out how long she'd be away. And when she got home, she'd find him waiting. Then they'd take things from there. If she didn't call, he'd head to Houston first thing in the morning.

Yesterday, he'd gotten her number from directory assistance. If he didn't hear from her tonight, then tomorrow he'd give the number to his source of information and find out exactly where Harley lived.

5

MONA WALKED INTO the shop Monday morning wearing a swing tent top and skinny pegged pants in apple green and tangerine. Fruit-shaped earrings in the respective shapes and colors hung from each ear.

She spun a circle on the toes of her sling-back mules. "Well, what do you think?"

Harley watched Mona's hair settle into place with the same easy wave as her top. "It's a step away from the Oriental drag queen, but I'm not sure in what direction."

Mona propped one retro-sixties outfitted hip on the corner of Harley's desk. "I have suffered a nervous breakdown and emerged unscathed. Bring on the breakfast."

"Hold that thought," Harley ordered and stepped into the recessed alcove around the corner from her desk.

She returned with a tray bearing croissants, bagels, muffins and toast, along with butter, cream cheese and raspberry jam. Setting the tray on her desk, she reached for a second platter laden with a Limoges tea service and a steeping pot of Earl Grey.

"Well," Mona began. Lips pursed, she touched her finger to the banana glaze drizzled down the side of one muffin, then pinched off a blueberry and popped it onto her tongue. "I think I'll fall apart more often."

Harley reached for a poppy-seed bagel. "Are things better with you and Gibson?"

"Let's just say Gibson has a lot on his mind."

"Such as shopping for matching wedding bands?"

"Gibson doesn't do jewelry."

"Then how about two tickets for a honeymoon cruise?"

"Let's just say Gibson is reconsidering whether he prefers to have his mid-life crisis or me."

"Ah, an ultimatum."

"I prefer to think of it as chaos management." Mona split open the muffin, then frowned when she caught sight of the suitcase tucked in the kneehole of Harley's desk. "You did it, didn't you? Spent Sunday reading the trade rags just like I said you would."

"Only until noon. Then I went shopping. And...made a couple of phone calls."

Mona's eyes widened theatrically. "You called him back."

"Saturday night, Sunday morning *and* Sunday evening." Harley dipped a knife in the cream cheese and dotted her bagel half. "I'm going to die when I get my phone bill."

Mona waved off the complaint. "Weekend rates are but pennies."

"Yeah, my pennies."

"Think of it as an investment in your future. I'm sure he's worth every hundred-dollar bill." Mona meowed, closing her lips around her muffin.

Harley smiled to herself, absently reaching for another scoop of cream cheese. "He said pretty close to the same thing."

"Not lacking in self-confidence, is he?"

"Or sex appeal. Or apparently money. Mona, he talked about sending his kid brother to A & M to study veterinary medicine." Harley slapped the knife back and forth across her bagel. "He didn't even stutter over the cost. He just stated it as a fact of life."

"Hmmm." Mona chewed, then poured two cups of tea. "First he's gorgeous. And now he's rich. When are you going to see him again?"

"If I see him again it won't be anytime soon. I'm off to Fredericksburg for an auction tomorrow. I thought I'd spend a few days checking the out-of-the-way shops around Austin and San Antonio."

Declining Mona's offer of cream, Harley lifted her cup and blew across the steaming surface. "Mrs. Mitchmore called this morning and wants me to look for a linen tablecloth. Are you up to holding down the fort for the rest of the week?"

"Why wouldn't I be?"

"You didn't sound too great last time I talked to you."

"That was before Gibson dropped by and reminded me why his senior class voted him Most Likely to Succeed Without Trying."

Harley couldn't help it. "Do I need to be on the lookout for a crib?"

"No, but you might want to pick up a suitable bridesmaid dress. I know how you love old clothes."

"Almost as much as you hate them." Harley couldn't remember ever smiling a bigger smile. She pulled Mona into a fierce hug. "I can't believe it. The man who doesn't believe in the arcane tradition of marriage finally popped the question."

"Well, not exactly," Mona mumbled into Harley's ear.

Drawing back, Harley asked, "What do you mean, 'not exactly'?"

"The only thing that popped was Gibson's jaw when it hit the ground. He has a much better understanding now of why I was voted Most Likely to Win in a Battle of Wills."

"Now why doesn't that surprise me?"

"What can I say? I love the man. He loves me."

"But you want him to put his money where his mouth is."

"Exactly. If he wants me to invest the rest of my life in his mid-life crisis—not to mention sacrificing my lithe and lovely body," Mona added with a dramatic shimmy, "he'd better be willing to make the same commitment."

"Well said. And well executed." Harley applauded loudly, wondering how the human race had managed to survive so long between battles of wills and mid-life crises.

"Listen, I'd better be off. I left the number of the bed-and-breakfast where I'll be staying right here," she said, indicating a slip of paper tucked into one of two dozen cubbyholes in the desk. "I'll call you when I get there tonight."

"Are you going to be calling anyone else tonight?"

"I thought about it," Harley admitted, lowering her cup and saucer to the desk.

Mona licked her fingers clean of muffin crumbs and glaze. "I believe that Fredericksburg is quite close to Gardner's area code."

"I thought about that, too."

"And if you're staying in a bed-and-breakfast it's sure to have nice sun-dried sheets and fluffy pillows and a huge feather bed. Just the way you like it."

"How do you know what I like?"

"I've worked with you for four years, Harley. If it disgusts me, you'll love it."

"That works in reverse, you know. You with the black-tiled bath and speakeasy bedroom."

"What kind of bedroom do you think Gardner Barnes has?" Mona asked, her gaze glazed and dreamy.

"He has an antique four-poster and a candlewick quilt."

"A match made in heaven." Mona clasped her hands to her chest, then narrowed one sharp eye. "How do you know so much about his bed? Harley, did you have phone sex?"

Harley felt her blush rise from the inside out. "No. Not really. But he asked me about my bed so I asked him about his."

"What else did he ask you?"

"Only about my nightgown. You know, that one Everly sent?"

"You mean that strappy piece of sin and sex?"

She nodded. "And I told him about the sheets."

"Not the—"

"Yes, the pink-and-black ones."

"Oh, Harley, what must he think. First the Evan Picone suit and now Victoria's Secret. You've given him everything a man wants. From sophistication to sluttery."

"Sluttery?"

"You know what I mean. Did you ask him about the Excalibur thing?"

"No, but I did ask him how many times he's pulled this business-card number."

"And?"

"He said I was his first."

"The man wants you. I knew it." Mona reached for Harley's suitcase. "What are you waiting for? Get going. I'll call the bed-and-breakfast and tell them you'll need coffee for two."

"You'll do no such thing," Harley ordered, eyeing the inch of cream cheese she'd slathered on her bagel. She set it down with disgust.

They walked out the back door of the shop into the narrow alleyway where Harley parked her Blazer. She climbed behind the wheel, adjusting the cuffed hem of her denim shorts before she shut the door. "Call me if you get any special requests while I'm gone."

"Don't worry." Mona set the suitcase behind Harley's seat. "I plan to sell you out of a job so you can retire in the manner to which you deserve to become accustomed."

Harley blinked at Mona's convoluted logic. "And who's going to provide this life-style of the rich and famous?"

"Gardner Barnes, of course."

Harley started the engine and put the truck in gear. "Maybe if I can interest him in a couple of my most expensive pieces I can retire on my own terms."

"Boring, Harley, boring. You have no sense of adventure. You need someone to retire with you and show you how to have fun."

Harley thought of the adventure she was taking with Gardner right now. "I don't know, Mona. I might just surprise you."

I've certainly surprised myself, she thought, driving off with a backward wave.

AFTER MAKING an out-of-the-way stop in Boerne, Harley barely made it to Fredericksburg before dark. She grabbed a quick fast-food dinner, then quietly wandered the yard of the bed-and-breakfast where she was staying. From her vantage point beneath a huge spreading oak, she watched the setting sun color the sky with muted shades of pink and blue.

She breathed deep, wondering what it would be like to live without traffic noises or smog. And then she thought of Gardner, which wasn't a complete surprise.

Though she'd insisted on not knowing what he did to make a living, he'd let slip the fact that he ran the family business. Did that mean he still lived in the one-horse town he'd grown up in? And, if so, what about the town? Had it changed with the times, or was it as small now as it had been then?

Harley walked toward the house. She climbed the first porch step, then stopped. Leaning back against a beam, she closed her eyes and absorbed the unpressured silence. As calming as she found the temporary lack of hustle, she didn't know if she could live anywhere but the city—not that Gardner had asked her to.

But if she were going to move this relationship forward—which seemed to be the consensus of her senses—she had to be prepared to deal with their differences. For as compatible as they might be in her fantasy, reality lasted a lot longer than dreams.

She knew Gardner was nothing like Brad. Loyalty was as much a part of Gardner as his looks. As important as he considered the first, the second meant nothing to him. That combination of values and virility made for a tempting package.

Yet, after the fantasy she'd woven last night, she hesitated calling this evening. He'd taunted her with an erotic dare, and she'd responded like a 1-900 late-night call. What if he told her not to call again?

Suddenly, that answer was unacceptable. Though they'd never met "properly," what they'd shared in conversation was the intimacy of lovers. He'd lifted her dragging spirits, done wonders for the pieces of her self-worth still suffering damage from Brad, and their verbal foreplay left her achingly frustrated.

Theirs held the easy comfort of a longtime relationship, as well as the tense adjustments to one new, and frighteningly intense. She was ready to take a giant leap for womanhood. Or for herself, anyway. She wanted to give Gardner a chance, and in doing so would be taking the biggest one of her life.

In the privacy of her room, she pulled her calling card from her purse. Climbing into the big feather bed, she propped the phone on her lap and snuggled back into a mountain of green, pink and yellow chintz and gingham pillows. Her hand trembled on the receiver.

"Harley," he stated, his voice cutting into the second ring. Warmth swept through her at the sound of her name on his tongue.

"Am I that predictable?" she asked with a laugh.

He chuckled. "You sound like that doesn't make you too happy."

"A woman I work with tells me that I need to get a life."

"Do you?"

Harley thought of Mona with affection. "Could be. She's been predicting my every move for a while now."

"Sounds like she knows you pretty well."

"Better than just about anybody."

"We could remedy that, you know." He paused, then cruised smoothly forward. "Unless you're still not ready."

Harley let his voice roll through her before she answered. "No. I think I am."

"What changed your mind?"

"I haven't been getting a lot of sleep lately."

"We could lose a lot of sleep together, if you tell me where you are."

Tonight she figured it was a safe enough reveal. "I'm in Fredericksburg." When he didn't respond, she added, "Texas."

"Yeah. I know where it is. I thought you were on a business trip."

Harley detected a frown in his voice. "I am. I'm attending an auction here tomorrow."

"How long are you going to be there?"

"I'm not really sure. I've cleared my schedule through the end of the week. If I don't find what I need in Fredericksburg tomorrow, I'll look someplace else."

Though it was a minute in coming, Gardner's answering laugh was supremely male, powerful and dangerous to most every part of her body. She toed off her sneakers and tucked her legs beneath her, folding herself around the awesome feeling.

"Don't worry about tomorrow, Harley. I know you're going to find exactly what you need."

"You know that much about me, huh?"

"I know a lot. Remember, I'm your fantasy."

Yes. He was. He certainly was. "I don't think that's exactly the way I put it."

"Close enough. Besides, after last night, I know more than you probably wish I did."

Harley pressed a palm to her cheek. "Gardner. About last night—"

He cut her off with, "Don't even try to take a word of it back."

"Then you're not disgusted?"

"Disgusted? Are you kidding?"

Harley shrugged for her own benefit. "After I hung up, I felt . . . I don't know . . . cheap."

He blew out an exasperated sigh. "Harley, cheap would be if you did that for a living. Or for some warped sense of sexual power. But I asked you to. You did it for me. Didn't you?"

Her stomach knotted and she pictured him close, his hand spreading over her belly to ease the flow of fire through her blood. "Yes. It was for you."

"Good. That's all I wanted to know." She imagined him pacing, scrubbing a hand over his hair. "What you and I say to each other in private is no one's business but our own. We can be as intimate, as personal, hell, as erotic as we want, as long as you know that the talking's not going to hold me much longer. Agreed?"

"On one condition."

"Name it."

"That you'll respect me in the morning," she said and held her breath.

"Oh, I'll respect you, Harley," he answered, the words an intimate stroke to her senses. "Especially after the night."

"The night?"

"Yeah. Night. You know, those hours of dark between dusk and dawn." His voice had shifted, grown subtly lower, a swirl of heat like rising steam, and the slow ebbing tide of her blood.

"I know about night," she finally replied.

"And you know about secrets. And desires. Have I ever told you *my* fantasy? What happens with you and me? At night?"

Harley swallowed hard. "No. You haven't."

"All pretenses come down, Harley. All walls, all defenses. You and me. And nothing else."

"You make it sound too easy," she managed, making a true effort at a false laugh.

"It's simple, Harley. As easy as one plus one. We start with the night, then slow and easy add the secrets—"

Her heart stopped, then started; her breathing came in choppy gasps.

"Next comes desires. Then you. And finally me—"

"What happens then?" she asked, her voice a mere whisper over the roar in her head.

"You've got a quick mind, Harley. Your calculations can't be far off from mine."

That's what she was afraid of. And what she wanted. Even knowing nothing more about him than she did, she wanted Gardner Barnes with the fiercest intensity.

"I don't have much of a mind for math. Why don't you just give me the answer?"

"That's cheating, Harley. Do I seem like that kind of guy?"

She hoped not. Oh, God, she hoped not. "Wouldn't be the first time I've been fooled."

Gardner took a minute to reply. "Honesty is either a part of a man or it isn't. If that's what happened to you, I'm sorry. You deserve better."

"How do you know what I deserve?" she asked, her voice slightly raw.

"No one deserves to be cheated on."

"I don't think the cheater took the cheated-on's feelings into the equation. In his case, one plus one wasn't enough. Or maybe I wasn't enough woman." She blew up a puff of breath, her bangs fluttering back over her forehead. "I'm sorry. I didn't call to dredge up the past."

"Why did you call?"

"To find out what we're going to do with the present."

"The present, huh? You mean, like maybe a real date."

She twisted the phone cord around her finger. "I know we've got some obstacles, like time and distance and schedules—"

"Those obstacles are nothing, Harley, now that we've gotten past the biggest one."

"You mean me."

"You needed time. I can understand that, but whatever caused you to change your mind I'm damn glad it happened."

She was damn glad, too. Anticipation was a giddy thing, and she felt its tiny fingers and toes start the climb up her backbone. "What do you like to do on a date, Gardner Barnes?"

"I don't remember."

"Seriously?"

"Seriously."

"Your imagination must be a little rusty."

"I'm not lacking in imagination," he growled. "Just opportunity. Why don't you give me your idea of a great date. I don't want to disappoint you."

She could talk to him for hours and never be disappointed. The realization seized her suddenly, giving her no time to weigh the implications.

"Think back to school, Gardner. I'm not a whole lot different from any of the girls you found time to date. Just a little older." And a whole lot wiser, she thought wryly. "I like to be romanced. I like flowers, dark corner tables with candlelight, having my car door opened and my chair pulled out."

"The last time I opened a door for a woman, she jerked the handle from my hand and told me she could do it herself."

"So can I. But those tiny shows of tenderness and respect mean a lot to me as a woman. I may be working in a man's world, but that doesn't make me a man. I'm too young to have burned my bra, but I wouldn't have, anyway. I enjoy the differences that make me a woman." *And screw Brad for being such a jerk and making me wonder why I wasn't woman enough.*

"That's some kind of sermon."

Harley cringed. "I'm sorry."

"Don't be. I like a woman who's a woman, who can stand up to a man without becoming one. A woman's strengths are totally her own. That's what makes the traditional roles so great."

She'd wanted so hard to believe in traditional roles, hard enough to take Brad at face value, hoping to find with him what she'd not found on the back of a Harley-Davidson with her arms wrapped tight around her mother's waist.

"Harley?"

"Hmmm? I was just thinking. You know, Gardner, if you're that big on traditional, you need to be the one to plan this date."

"It'll be my pleasure," he said, his words rolling out on a prayer and a promise.

Pleasure and Gardner Barnes. Harley couldn't begin to imagine. "Do you want to meet me somewhere on the road? Or should we wait until I get back to Houston so we can better coordinate our schedules?"

"I don't know if I can deal with all this spontaneity, Harley."

She easily pictured his sexy grin. "Then the next time you pull this business-card routine, why don't you check out a girl's area code first?"

"If there's ever a need for a next time, I won't bother with a business card. I'll just stake my claim and be done with it."

"Is that what this is? Staking your claim?"

"I'm giving it my damnedest."

"Then you tell me the when and where and I'll make my damnedest effort to be there."

"Who's staking claims now?"

"You got a problem with that, Barnes?"

"Not a one. Call me when you get ready to leave Fredericksburg. I'll see what I can do about setting up this date."

"Until tomorrow, then?"

"Yeah. Tomorrow." He said it with such potential that Harley shivered. "And, Harley?"

"Yeah, Gardner?"

"I'm glad you didn't burn your bra. I'm going to enjoy taking it off."

"SOLD!"

Damn, she'd wanted that nightgown. The final item in the auction and the only thing she'd wanted for herself. Figured. She'd arrived early, set up her folding chair in one of the center rows, then walked through the barn, scouting out the items to be auctioned before she picked up her bidding card from the cashier. She would have been on the road long before now if she hadn't had her heart set on the simple linen shift.

Harley glanced over her shoulder, but the crush of people prevented her from locating the jerk who'd had the gall to have more money than she did. Spending clients' money gave her a vicarious thrill, because when it came to spending her own, she had to set a more frugal limit. Damn, she'd wanted that nightgown.

At least Dr. Fischer should be a happy man. The earthenware inhaler and the mahogany pill-making machine were the best quality she'd seen in a long time. A few more choice items such as those, and her deal with Dr. Fischer would be a fait accompli. Pulling her check register and a business card from her briefcase, she made her way to the cashier's table.

The antique business was getting tougher, especially with the choicest antiques owned by museums or affluent collectors. She often wondered if owners were holding back their best items, and from discussions with other dealers, she was not alone in her concern. Collectors were going to have to get used to the new generation of antiques coming up. Harley had gone so far as to start her own collection of teapots in addition to her treasured assortment of old clothes.

Once she'd tendered payment, she arranged to have the items shipped directly to her store, preferring to pay the insurance and shipping on the parcels, rather than risk damaging them in the back of her four-wheel drive.

She'd had no luck finding Mrs. Mitchmore's linens, however, and no matter how inviting the idea of lingering in town long enough to call Gardner, she needed to be on her way. She'd call him from wherever she managed to stop tonight. Their date would just have to wait.

Even as she mentally voiced the words, a pang of regret slipped up on her better judgment. Funny how she'd always thought of these buying trips as a challenge. This one was growing to be a chore.

"Excuse me," she murmured, skirting her way past two older women arguing over the price one had paid for a Snoopy cookie jar. Just as Harley stepped past, the first woman turned to the side and opened her satchel.

The handle loops caught on the corner of Harley's briefcase, jerking her shoulder back, and yanking the purse from the woman's grasp. A Mary Poppins array of books, brass knickknacks, buttons, beer bottle crowns, an envelope of stamps, an old Barbie doll and a lead doorstop tumbled to the ground.

"Now look here, Helen. I told you that purse was going to be the death of you," scolded the second woman, standing above the kneeling Helen and shaking her finger.

Helen took on the look of a wounded child, the slashes of rouge over her cheekbones nothing compared to the red cast creeping up her neck.

Harley dropped down beside her. "It's my fault, really. This briefcase is too bulky for such tight quarters."

"That's all right, miss. Ellen's always telling me to leave things in the car, but I'm afraid someone will break in and steal them." A small crowd had gathered now, chasing buttons and bottle caps through the dirt-and-sawdust floor.

Harley picked up the Barbie doll and dusted cedar flakes from its platinum hair. "Don't worry about it, Helen. We'll get it all gathered up." She handed her the doll. "Is this for your granddaughter?"

"No, that's not for her granddaughter," Ellen butted in. A wiry bird of a woman, Ellen fluttered from side to side and flapped her skinny arms. "She's got bookcases full of dolls in her trailer house. Dolls on top of the TV, on top of the refrigerator. Dolls on her dresser."

Helen gave a little shrug. "I like dolls."

"I tell you what, Helen," Harley said, nodding toward the Barbie. "You take care of this one. She's going to be worth something someday. Now let's get the rest of these buttons up."

Harley, Helen and Ellen took bottle caps and buttons out of several hands. Harley leaned forward and reached for a small brass Empire State Building ashtray behind Helen's left foot, only to be knocked off balance by someone at her back.

She shuffled one foot, then scooted on the other, and made a grab for the denim-covered thigh crouched down beside her to keep from pitching on her face.

"Thanks," she said, righting herself and turning to the side.

"You're welcome," said an all-too-familiar voice, and Harley found herself gazing into the bedroom eyes of Gardner Barnes.

6

THE FIRST TIME she'd seen him, she'd had on three-inch pumps; he'd been wearing Italian loafers. That had to be the reason he hadn't seemed as tall then as he did now.

On the plane they hadn't stood this close, so close he filled every inch of her vision. That had to be why she didn't remember his chest being as broad beneath navy silk as it was now under white chambray.

But try as she might, she couldn't come up with any rational explanation for the man to look so sexy, so breathtakingly magnificent, so utterly male. And that was exactly the way he looked now.

Even when he stepped closer, so close she had to tilt back her head, she couldn't look away from his eyes. Eyes she didn't remember being this green, sparkling with this much life—or fire. He blinked slowly, lazily, the easy sweep of his long dark lashes at odds with the banked emotion behind.

The peripheral movement of his arm was more a feeling than an image, the flex of a shoulder, the crinkle of crisp cotton. Trembling, Harley breathed in the scent of soap and sun-kissed cloth, and waited for his touch.

His breath stirred the wisps of unmanageable hair curling at her temple, the contact no more than a stroke of air on skin. Harley shivered, hunched deep into the turned-up collar of her belted wrap, and waited.

Angling his head toward her, Gardner reached up, trailed his thumb along her lower lip, tugging on the center until she wet the spot with a flick of her tongue.

"Cat got your tongue, Harley Golden?"

No, but you do, she thought. His flavor filled her mouth. She spoke the first words that floated through her mind. "I didn't know you were a cowboy."

His knuckles grazed her jawline; his huge palm sizzled against her neck; his fingers speared into the hair behind her ear. "Does that matter to you?"

Not only did it not matter, but from the moment their eyes had made contact, the rest of her world had ceased to exist. Instinctively, she shook her head.

"Good." The brim of his Resistol cast an intimate shadow over her face. "Because I don't think I can wait any longer."

The warmth of his smile tickled her cheek. Her breasts tingled, her blood thrummed and Harley felt as if she'd been waiting forever.

Sliding his hand from her neck down her shoulder, Gardner wrapped his fingers possessively around her upper arm and backed a step away.

With the return of her space, came her sanity. Harley shook off her daze to the murmur of voices and the sounds of shuffling chairs, rustling paper and hammers on nails. Never in her life had she lost all awareness at a single touch.

Gardner Barnes was a dangerous man.

Still, she went with him willingly. His insistent pace gave no quarter to the flurried beating of her heart. The man qualified as aerobic activity. Her pulse rate had reached optimum level and she'd barely flexed a muscle.

They cleared the barn door in a matter of seconds and Harley blinked at the sudden glare of the sun. Gardner didn't say a word, but neither did she. She couldn't. Her senses were a riot, a whirlwind, a crazy jumble of perceptions. With nothing but his hand on her arm, he had reduced her to a bundle of frenzied nerves.

Wrong, Harley. Your jitters started about the time he gave you that be-my-love-slave look. Or when he said so much in so few words. A basket case, that's what she was. A basket case waiting to happen.

Her denim skirt swirled around her calves. Her briefcase bounced against her hip. And, even through the cotton fibers of her Navajo-patterned wrap, Gardner's hand was warm against her arm.

He guided her around the corner of the barn, down the side, past a stack of straw-filled shipping crates in view of nothing but a sliver of the graveled parking lot and the rolling expanse of central Texas hills.

Then the barn wall was behind her, Gardner's hands splayed flat on either side of her head. Two feet of tense air seethed between their bodies. His eyes blazed with green fire; his chest rose and fell with short choppy breaths.

And the denim-covered promise straining the zipper of his jeans told her all she needed to know of his fight for control.

Harley dropped her forgotten briefcase at her feet. A heady rush of feminine power chased desire through her blood. He wanted her, and wasn't ashamed to let her see exactly how much.

She touched her tongue to her upper lip. "How did you find me?"

"You told me where you were," he said, grinding his jaw.

The tic of the muscle along his ear beat in meter with the pounding in Harley's blood. "I didn't think—"

"Shhh." He laid two fingers over her lips. "I said I'm through talking. Remember?"

Moving her lips against the rough pads of his fingers, she barely managed a nod because, as he'd talked, he'd stepped closer.

"Good." He withdrew his hand and touched her with his gaze. Only his gaze. First her face, then the length of her body, his heated glance lingering below her waist where she held her hands together.

"Lord, you're gorgeous." He smiled then, and raised his head. "And you're nervous, aren't you?"

"A little." What an understatement. Her anxiety was so obvious she didn't know why he'd asked. But the play of her nerves wasn't as much hesitation or anxiety as frustration and desire. She didn't want to make a wrong move and destroy a chance at something she so desperately wanted.

His wrists hovered at her jawline; his hands on the wall supported his weight. With every ragged breath he took, his chest imperceptibly grazed hers. He spread his legs cowboy wide, and the denim of his jeans scraped the denim of her skirt.

Harley wanted to close all those distances—and more. To press her body against the solid length of his. To fulfill the promise of this first encounter. To take them both to a place where differences and pasts and futures didn't matter.

What Harley wanted was her forgotten dream. Her illusion of perfect life. One man. One woman. Forever.

His glittering gaze held her immobile. And then he lowered his head, touched her with nothing but the faintest brush of his mouth. It wasn't the first taste she wanted. So she gripped the mountainous muscles of his shoulders, stepped in closer and parted her lips.

His flavor came from the earth, pure, unseasoned and male. His scent teased her, the fragrance a mix of fresh air and clean skin and . . . and Gardner. His was an aroma dark and potent, as elemental as the sun, as primitive as the land. She detected no hint of the shallow, artificial man she'd once thought he might be. And she was glad.

Needing more, she opened wider, teasing the seam of his lips with her tongue. She laid her palms against his chest, the muscles she touched honed to cowboy perfection, and not from hours spent training in the gym. This man made his living with his body. He was a man in a way Brad could never understand. A man who challenged her deepest spirit of womanhood.

She welcomed the gauntlet, sliding her hands up the starched chambray to encircle his neck. With the press of her fingertips at his nape, the slide of her tongue along the sweet length of his, Harley told him how she felt, how she wanted him.

Oh, how she wanted him. She wanted him until she ached, until she couldn't be sure where passion left off and necessity began. She rubbed tiny circles at his hairline, pressed her body fully against his. The movements displayed her juxtaposed feelings, equal in sentiment, diametric in urgency.

Gardner responded by shifting the kiss, in position and in tone, frantically lifting the hem of her skirt. Cupping her bottom in his palms, he bunched the denim in his fists until it grazed the top of her boots, the backs of her knees, her lower thighs.

She parted her legs at the gentle nudge of air against her skin, and at the insistent search of Gardner's fingers. His need to get close was a tangible thing.

It was Harley's need, too. And it was eating her up.

He'd given her four days of visions and wild imaginings, all of it leading to this. His mouth on hers, his breath hot against her hotter skin. Her nipples peaked, begging. She clenched her thighs beneath his questing hands.

He tore his mouth away. The stubble on his jaw abraded her cheek. "This isn't enough, Harley."

"Yes." Was it a breath? A promise? An unconscious invitation? No matter. Gardner seemed to know. He moved his hands to her waist and lifted her to sit on the nearest crate. He tossed his hat behind.

Without a word spoken, his mouth returned to hers, his hands on her knees pushing her skirt high on her legs. His fingers found the bare skin of her thighs and a groan rolled up his throat.

Harley struggled to get closer, the kiss all but forgotten. Her hands flexed, pulling at his shirt. He parted her legs and Harley opened wider; he stepped between and she scooted home.

Her lips were bruised and his were damp as he settled them against the base of her neck, but the wetness was nothing compared to the slick heat he would find should he touch her.

And she wanted him to touch her. To take her. To ease the ache she'd lived with since the first time they'd talked on the phone. He slid his hands beneath her skirt, up her thighs to her waist, hooked his fingers in the band of her panties.

She lifted her hips and he rolled the scrap of satin and lace down her legs and over her boots. With his hands spread along her upper thighs, his thumbs in the crease where her hips met her legs, he teased the nest of curls between, and Harley knew she was ready.

Hugging his waist, she palmed his buttocks, the backs of his thighs. The muscle tensed and flexed beneath her touch. Responding to her. For her. Harley wanted to cry out, soaring with the power she held in her hands.

She slipped her fingers under the waistband of his jeans and grazed the skin beneath his Fruit of the Looms. This is madness, she told herself, reaching for his belt buckle. Wild and crazy, she added, moving to his button fly. She didn't know this man at all, yet she knew him completely.

So when he closed his hand over her shaking fingers and stopped her, she wasn't totally surprised.

"This is insane, Harley." He breathed his echo of her sentiment across the kiss-dampened skin of her throat.

"I know," she murmured.

"We have to stop."

"I know." What was she saying? What was *he* saying?

"Now, Harley. I can't do ... I don't have ... Dammit, Harley. Stop."

Harley stiffened, pulling back all the emotion floating around her like sunlight. She jerked at his hold, trying to free her hands. She wanted to push him away and make a beeline for her Blazer before the red flush of humiliation spread all the way to her face.

She'd thrown herself at him like a cowboy groupie of the worst kind and he'd roped her advance to a halt. He didn't want her, but he still wouldn't let her go. A muffled cry spilled from her throat.

"Harley."

He released her hands and she scrambled to pull down her skirt. Then he took her by the shoulders, moved one hand gently to her chin.

"Harley, look at me."

Reluctantly, she did. His eyes had lost none of their fire. The tendons on his neck stood in rigid relief beneath his bronzed skin.

"I didn't mean for this to go so far so fast. And I don't have a condom." He stroked his thumb over her cheekbone, his smile gentle, his eyes kind. "You do crazy things to me, Harley Golden. You make me lose my mind. And you deserve better than a quick grope on a shipping crate."

Harley lowered her lashes. Damn her blush-happy complexion. "I thought . . . I wasn't sure . . ."

"About what?" he asked, trailing the tips of his fingers down her neck.

Desperately, she searched for an answer, but her mind was a muddled mess. Gardner's fingers had drifted lower. Lower still. "You stopped me. I wasn't sure if—"

"If what? I wanted you?"

He'd reached the deep V of her neckline now, the point a good two inches lower than normal due to the loosened belt at her waist. He leaned forward, dipped his tongue in her cleavage, then moved up to nuzzle the base of her neck in a possessive kiss.

"You thought I'd changed my mind?" He laved the bruised skin with a healing lick of his tongue, then drifted higher and bit her again.

He was eating her alive. That had to mean he wanted her. Harley arched into him and told her old wounds to take a hike.

"Give me your hand," he ordered.

She did, and, though shocked at the initial contact, allowed him to press her palm firmly to his arousal.

"This is how much I want you." He cupped her fingers around the rigid length. "But this sure as hell isn't where I want it to happen. And it will happen." He squeezed her hand around him, ground himself against her palm, then let her go. "You know that, don't you?"

Mouth dry, she nodded.

Bending down, he scooped up her panties and her briefcase. The briefcase he handed over. The panties he tucked into his back pocket. "Then let's get the hell out of here."

Boosting her down off the crate, he reached behind her for his hat, laced her fingers tightly through his, then headed toward the front of the barn.

Cognizance returned long enough for her to realize the parking lot had nearly emptied. Shadowy figures moved through the barn, cleaning, straightening. Gardner never stopped to look back. He never said a word. His sights were set on a crew cab pickup parked at a crooked slant against the fence on the far side of her Blazer.

He suddenly seemed to take measure of their two-vehicle situation. He stopped abruptly, bringing Harley up short. Tilting his head to one side, he asked, "Is that your Blazer?"

She nodded and managed a tremulous smile, the moment still thick with the tension of what had passed between them—and where they were headed.

"C'mon," he said and took off again like a shot. Once there, Harley produced her keys from the briefcase with a minimal show of nerves. She climbed into the seat and Gardner loomed over her in the open door, one hand propped on the roof, one gripping the doorframe.

He stared down at her, his gaze intense and burning with so much life that she couldn't resist the urge to reach up and kiss the sun-dimpled corner of his eye. He smiled then.

And Harley fell in love.

"You said you'd cleared your schedule to the end of the week." He toyed with a lock of her hair, rubbing the strands between his thumb and forefinger with intense concentration. "Spend the time with me."

"Here?"

He shook his head and looked up. "At my ranch."

She offered him a private smile. "Is this ranch your family business?"

"One and the same." Tucking her hair behind her ear, he asked, "Where are you staying?"

"At a bed-and-breakfast on Main Street."

"Then I'll follow you back and wait while you pack your things."

"Is this our date?" she asked.

A grin, dazzling in its innocent charm, broke across his mouth. "I guess it is."

Harley forced a pout. "A girl likes to be romanced, Gardner. Not ordered around."

He patted his shirt pockets. "I'm fresh out of flowers and diamonds, Harley."

"Then I'll settle for a 'pretty please.'"

He dropped to one knee—actually dropped to one knee—removed his hat and took her hand in his. "Harley Golden, would you do me the honor of spending the rest of the week with me?"

"Not bad, Barnes."

"Well?" He settled his hat back in place. "I'm waiting here."

"I'd love to," she said, wishing in some renegade part of her heart that he'd asked something else, and she'd answered the same.

Gardner got to his feet. With a brief nod he indicated the crew cab doolie parked twenty feet away. "I need to return the truck I borrowed. We can leave your Blazer at the airstrip."

"The airstrip?"

"Yeah. It's where I left the Cessna." He leaned forward and kissed her, his mouth a consuming presence.

Then he slammed the door and walked away, his stride long legged and determined, his shoulders broad and capable of carrying a family's weight.

The man owned a Cessna, used diamonds and flowers interchangeably, planned to put his kid brother through veterinary school.

And the white flag fluttering from his back pocket was her panties.

SHE WASN'T SURE which was worse. Death from sexual frustration or sexual excitement.

A quick grope on a shipping crate sounded like heaven to Harley.

She reached for her gown. Halfway through the folding, she stopped, and draped the blush-tone concoction of film and froth over her arm. The sheer lace breathed over her skin, gently roused the hairs on her arms.

Eyes closed, Harley succumbed, hearing the whisper-soft sounds of sheer chiffon against Fruit of the Looms, hair-dusted male skin, crisp sheets, a hardwood floor. Desire unfurled deep and low, then spiraled upward in an airy rush of bliss.

A cowboy. A ride-'em-and-rope-'em, range-bred, tight-jeaned, park-your-boots-under-my-bed cowboy. She'd never even dreamed.

Once they'd left the auction barn, Gardner had followed her to the bed-and-breakfast. His big truck loomed large in her rearview mirror, an intimidating, intoxicating presence, bearing down. A hunter, a predator, a man in pursuit of his woman.

She was his woman. And he was waiting outside, hat brim low, back snugged up to the wide-trunked oak, thumbs hooked in his belt loops, leg cocked, boot heel flush with the tree's base. Harley stepped away from the foot of the bed, lifted one edge of the scalloped curtain and frowned.

At least he'd been waiting there when she'd hurried inside to pack not thirty minutes ago.

She knew he wasn't leaving without her. He'd made that point perfectly, eloquently clear. Staking his claim with strong hands and an eager tongue, he'd backed away from the doorway of her parked Blazer, his eyes bright, his lips glistening with the remnants of her kiss, and told her she had half an hour.

Harley touched her tongue to her upper lip, slicked it over her lower. Um-hmm. The man definitely knew how to kiss. A week of such kisses was a daunting thought. A week of where his kisses could lead and . . . Harley shivered. No. She couldn't think about it.

Her traitorous body thought of nothing else.

The exquisite play of his callused fingers on the skin of her thighs. The delicious, and entirely too brief, flick of his tongue over the swell of her breast. His teeth, nibbling, his lips, suckling.

Trembling, her fingers found the reddish bruise at the base of her throat, and her hands remembered. The muscles of his chest, his shoulders, and the firm arousal he'd been so willing to share.

Damn. How was she going to make it through the rest of the week?

Heavy steps trod on the tongue-and-groove oak flooring of the parlor outside her door. Boot steps. Headed her way. Louder. Then dead silence. The crystal doorknob turned; the hinges creaked. Harley clutched the nightgown to her chest and forgot to breathe.

Gardner stepped into the room. The door gave a click of finality as he eased it closed.

The room's temperature soared, and Harley's heart was a wild pump of muscle, priming her body for possession by the green-eyed cowboy not ten feet away.

He removed his Resistol, turned it crown down on the glass top of the black iron table tucked up under the only window in the room. Then he reached into his pocket, and dropped her panties into the hat.

This room was definitely too small for two people. Harley couldn't move an inch without running into the air Gardner was breathing. So she stayed where she was, unmoving.

The air closed in, held her captive. And Gardner's gaze swallowed her whole.

"Finished packing?" He nodded toward the nightgown she still hugged like salvation.

She glanced around the room, frantically searching for a reason she was taking so long. A reason more tangible than the sheer enormity of the step she was taking.

Unable to find one, she held up the nightgown and smiled. "This is all I have left."

"Nice. I like it." He unhooked his belt buckle, slipped the belt from the loops, draped the leather strip over the headboard.

"I thought you were in a hurry to get back to the ranch," Harley managed.

"I am." He tossed a box of condoms on the bed. "But some things will wait. Some things won't."

"You mean . . ." She tilted her head toward the bed.

"Yeah. I mean." He gave a nod in the same direction, and popped the snaps of his chambray shirt. Balanced on one foot, he tugged off the opposite boot. It thunked against the floor, then boot number two joined its mate.

Harley's eyes widened at the wicked lift of his darkly arched brow. At the mischievous eyes sparkling with fire. At the sly curl of his lip. And the smile that enticed and seduced.

Gardner braced his hands at his lean waist, the tail of his shirt flaring wide. "Now let's get you out of those clothes."

7

"YOU WANT ME to take off my clothes?"

He nodded.

"Here?"

He nodded.

"Now?"

He nodded. It was all he could manage with Harley not ten feet away. Damn, but reality beat the pants off phone calls. "Do you need some help?"

"Do you want to help?"

"No," he croaked, making fists of both hands. "I'll watch."

"All right," she whispered and shrugged, tossing the gown toward the suitcase lying open on the rack.

The jacket moved with her, slipping from one shoulder, then the other. Sliding down her arms. Catching on her wrists. Hitting the floor with the sound of a sigh.

God, what breasts. Her simple white bra matched the panties in his hat. Her rib cage was narrow, her waist narrower still. And her breasts were what breasts should be. Plump, round, heavy. Perfect. She fumbled with the back hook, eased the straps from her shoulders and let the bra fall.

His lungs compressed. His veins constricted and cut off the flow of blood to his head. But not to his groin. His erection tested the durability of denim better than weeks in the saddle.

Harley smiled a tentative smile. With nervous fingers, she released the three buttons on the side of her skirt. Her breasts swung free; her nipples pouted, puckered and begged for attention. Gardner swallowed a gallon of saliva.

And then her skirt hit the floor.

Her hips were made to cradle a man, her legs to hold him once he came home. Her belly was flat, her sex hidden beneath a riot of curls he wanted to part with his tongue. Sweat pooled at the base of his throat. He couldn't move to wipe it away.

Harley Golden embodied everything female—from the mystery of innocence, to the madness of seduction, to the arousing potential to carry his child.

He backed up and sat in the room's single black wrought-iron chair. "C'mere."

She shook her head, chewed at her lower lip.

"Why not?" A tiny hint of apprehension nudged him. If she'd been teasing, he could've ignored it. She was serious.

"Promise not to laugh?" she finally asked, her expression uncertain.

"Why would I laugh?" He was so tense, a gust of breath and he'd snap.

Her tongue dotted her lip. "This is so stupid. I want to do this right."

She didn't know. She really didn't know. "Harley, honey, if you were any more right, I wouldn't be here now."

"You wouldn't?" She twisted her hands at her waist.

"I'd be buried, six feet under, with an epitaph that read, Here Lies Gardner Barnes. He Died Of A Broken Hard-On." She blushed, and he loved every red streak. "Now are you gonna come here?"

"You didn't promise not to laugh."

He made a bold capital X over his heart and she stepped around the foot of the bed . . . wearing nothing but leather boots.

Gardner had died and gone to rodeo heaven. "Come over here and ride me, city girl."

Her steps drowned out her cry of delight, then she was on his lap, straddling him. His hands cupped her bare bottom, his fingers searched out the warmth he'd wanted so long. His face found a home in the creamy valley he'd dreamed of forever.

He took one pink bud between his lips and Harley bowed her back. He sucked harder, filled his mouth with her taste, tugged with his lips, drew her deep inside.

"Gardner," she cried. "Stop. Please."

"Not a chance." He flicked one nipple, pinched the other.

"Please. Your shirt. I want it off."

She yanked at the snaps. Gardner reached between their bodies, and jerked the shirt from his jeans. Harley helped him slide it off.

Holding her plump breasts in his palms, Gardner dragged her nipples through the hair on his chest. Then Harley took over. Pushing his hands away, she held herself against him, moving skin against skin, virgin white against hardened bronze, pebbled female peaks against flat male discs.

Gardner glanced up, then wished he hadn't. How was he going to last? Eyes closed, Harley chewed on her lower lip, pouted and whimpered, and made throaty little moans. He couldn't help it. He thrust upward.

Sleepy and aroused, her bluebonnet eyes drifted open. She found him watching. Her lips parted, and he ached to be between, to feel them close around his...his tongue would have to do for now. He pulled her head down to his.

Her sweet little palms framed his face, holding him still for the motions of her mouth. Speaking with her tongue, her lips, with tiny nips of her teeth, she told him of her loneliness, her want, her ability to fulfill his desires.

Need devoured him, tearing at his soul, ripping at the answers, the plan he'd laid for his life, leaving jagged edges that only Harley could mend.

Then the kiss deepened. And her body moved. The gentle song of her spirit vanished. Rock 'n' roll hunger took its place. She ground her hips on the bulge in his jeans.

And Gardner was through playing.

"Wrap your legs around my waist." His hands stroked her bottom—stroked, explored and squeezed. Then in one clean motion he gained his feet. He backed her into the bed and fell into plump pillows, feathers and a quilt old enough to have seen decades of love.

His skin kissed hers from belly to breast. Braced on one arm, he gazed down. "I've got you where I want you, Harley Golden."

"You do?"

"Um-hmmm." He palmed her rib cage, just below one breast. "It can't get any better than this."

Harley trailed one finger down his breastbone. "I wouldn't think a man like you—" she'd reached his navel now "—would be satisfied with so little." She slipped her fingers behind the fly of his jeans. Her eyes brightened. "Especially when you have so *much* to give."

He'd kept his jeans on to last longer, but her sloe-eyed gaze turned his resolve into jelly. Everything else remained rock hard.

To hell with making this first time last. To hell with sweet nothings and skillful seduction. They'd had three days of extended foreplay. It was time for the fireworks. Gardner rolled over, shucked off both jeans and drawers.

And that's when he saw the hat. Floppy brimmed and hanging on the wall. A hat tucked full of flowers. And feathers. He smiled, plucked a bright yellow plume from the brim, then rolled back to Harley.

"Close your eyes," he ordered, parting her legs and kneeling between.

"No." Her hair fanned across the quilt like summer's wheat. "I want to see you."

At her soft words, her tone of awe, a proud and mighty surge of blood thickened his arousal. He let her look . . . until he thought he'd come from the impatience in her gaze.

He brushed the feather across her eyelids. "You've looked enough. Now I want you to feel."

"Gardner," she complained.

He silenced her with a stroke of down across her lips, then dusted each eye one more time. "Time's up, Harley. You've spent your quarter. No more looking. No more talking." His gaze skimmed her pliant body; his stomach rolled in hunger. "Now it's time to feel."

Gripping her hips, he pulled her toward him, placing the backs of her thighs high over his. Their positions afforded him a hell of a view; his condition allowed him the briefest enjoyment. This was going to be so good.

Sliding the ripe tip of his sex into her feminine folds, he drew the feather down her body in a line from breastbone to navel.

"Feel the difference. Soft." He circled each breast with the feather, then pushed his erection into her wet and waiting heat. "Hard."

He tangled the yellow fluff in the curls between her thighs. "Soft." Gut clenched, he entered her slowly, fully. Harley tightened around him. "Hard."

And getting harder. Why had he started this game?

Leaning forward, he touched the tip of his tongue to the peak of each rosy breast. "Feel the difference. Wet." He blew across the distended tips. "Dry."

Harley shivered.

"Cold." He licked her again, blew again. Then pushed into her, deep and hard. "Hot."

Grinding his jaw, he pulled out completely, eased back in, then withdrew. "Slow."

He was never going to last. Lifting her heels to his shoulders, he supported his weight on his palms, stretched his legs out behind him. His hunger set the tempo. "Fast."

Deliberately, he forced himself to slow. "Gentle." Then said to hell with it and let the demands of his body rule. "Rough."

Harley writhed beneath him. Insanity fired the animal sounds rushing up his throat. Sobs and whimpers spilled from between Harley's sweet lips. He took them with his own.

His hands went crazy, kneading, probing—but no more crazy than hers. Clinging, digging, her needy fingers gouged his back from shoulders to ribs. He wanted to crawl deep inside her and make her body a part of his.

He didn't want it to end. Ever.

Thighs clenched, he lowered their weight into the mattress. Harley wrapped her legs around his waist, her arms around his back and held him close. She opened her eyes and looked up.

"Sex," she said, squeezing him with muscles he'd driven deep to find. Then she took his mouth and mated her tongue with his. Long slow strokes. Wet and welcoming. Sizzling and sweet. Hot and wonderful and as intimate as the act itself.

Nipping his lower lip, Harley gentled the kiss and pulled back. "Making love."

That was all he needed to hear. His control was history.

With her boot heels digging crescents in his hips, Gardner rocked against her, rocked the bed off the wall and rocked himself home in the cradle of her body.

GARDNER BANKED the Cessna to the right, giving Harley a clear view of the green-and-brown patchwork fields that comprised the whole of Camelot. His home. His legacy.

He'd chosen his lifelong mistress well; Camelot's demands were harsh, but definable, their bond irrevocable—not one made of the capricious, temperamental knots in which his mother had bound his father in the name of love.

Gardner watched the sweep of land roll by, his pride a heady thing. Only Jud and Ty aroused his emotions more than the land. He loved his ranch with a passion of the heart, one he could never feel for a woman. No matter how much he wanted her.

And he wanted Harley Golden again, and again, a deeper want than he'd thought—feared—possible.

After they'd made it out of bed, Gardner had dressed and carried Harley's bags to his truck while Harley, insisting he not look, grabbed up her clothes and hustled into the bathroom. As if he hadn't seen everything. As if she hadn't given him more.

Looking as pulled together as a woman could wearing more whisker burns than clothes, she'd come back into the bedroom and demanded the return of her panties. He'd refused.

It was a small show of wills, but when he'd pulled her flush against him and shown her exactly why he liked her bottom bare, she'd acquiesced.

Together they'd ridden in silence to a private airstrip on the outskirts of town, the cab of the truck seeming smaller than Gardner had noticed on the drive in. Of course, then he'd been alone, not accompanied by one very sexy woman he knew inside out.

Fighting back the urge to stop the truck in the middle of the road and take Harley's sweetness once more, Gardner had returned the borrowed crew cab and arranged to have Harley's Blazer picked up and stored at the hangar.

Other than acknowledging his profession, Harley had made no comment regarding his wealth. She'd remained quiet, even in the air. But Gardner hadn't minded. The silence was comfortable. They didn't need conversation to communicate.

He pointed out the lay of the land, but she never glanced his way. Instead, she reached across the cabin and touched his thigh, the contact no more than a quick squeeze of affection.

It didn't matter. He wanted her again. He wanted to take it slow and easy, to talk to her about the future. But later. After they'd gotten beyond this stage of brushfire lust.

It might've been a better idea to contain his search for his children's mother closer to home. Women raised under ranching conditions knew the kind of life they were in for. But none of the available women he knew lit his fuse like Harley Golden.

Physically, their encounter in Fredericksburg was what first times should be, what first times rarely were. But he knew that, emotionally, Harley hadn't been sure how to deal with his unexpected arrival.

At the auction barn she'd been tense, uptight, not the Harley he'd grown to lo . . . grown fond of. In her room at the bed-and-breakfast, she'd been unsure of both herself and him.

Release was all he expected from sex. He'd thought that would be enough in his marriage. He wasn't so sure anymore. Harley altered beliefs he'd clung to for a lifetime when she demanded he make love.

Gardner turned his attention to the controls. Now they were home. The land looked fertile, the future loomed brighter. He had Harley at his side. The woman he wanted in his bed. And in his life.

The one who told him about growing up on a motorcycle and hating it. The one who felt disjointed, lost, disconnected from her family. The one who needed friends besides those who ate tofu for Christmas.

The one who wished someone other than her sister would give her sexy underwear. Who wanted someone other than a business associate to know her better than anybody.

A few of these things she'd told him. The rest he knew. He just knew. Because she was the Harley who would give his children love and laughter and blue-bonnet eyes.

"WELCOME TO CAMELOT." Tyler smiled up at Harley, a Lone Star Feed and Fertilizer bill cap pulled low on his brow.

Placing her hand in his uplifted palm, Harley swiveled in her seat and smiled at the younger, but no less devastating, Barnes family male. "You must be Tyler."

"The one and only," he answered, a grin to rival Gardner's in hunk appeal splitting his face. "And more competition than big brother cares to admit."

"I can see the resemblance in your e...go...oooo," Harley cried, airborne. Hands at her waist, Tyler whirled her through the air. Harley braced herself on his muscled shoulders. A gust of wind whipped up her skirt to her bare bottom.

Mortification followed, until she realized her skirt still hugged her knees.

"Tyler!" Gardner barked, and Tyler swung her to the ground.

"Looks like I'm in *big* trouble," Tyler exaggerated, his Gardner green eyes dramatically wide.

A true ham if Harley'd ever seen one.

Harley's bags in his hands, Gardner stomped around the rear of the plane. "If you can drag your hands away from Miss Golden, little brother, I could use 'em over here."

Tyler frowned down at his hands on her waist. He shook his head. "What can I say? They've got a mind of their own."

Thoroughly—though, she prayed not too obviously—charmed, Harley smoothed down her skirt once Tyler released her. "Maybe you should see a doctor about that."

"And miss all the fun?" Tyler tipped his hat, added a wink and jogged around to the back of the Rover.

"Damn, I'm glad I'm not that boy's father," Gardner muttered, shouldering past Harley with the armload of bags.

She paid no attention to his lie, but watched the two men wrestle her suitcases with an ease that came from a lifetime spent working side by side. And a camaraderie that spoke of friendship as much as brotherly love and respect.

A bittersweet smile tugged at her lips. It was the only outward show of emotion—regret? jealousy?—she allowed, refusing to indulge in melancholy when the immediate future held such potential.

Leaving Tyler to arrange the luggage, Gardner approached. This time Harley's smile was heartfelt and pure. He stopped two feet away. She resisted closing the distance. "Did you have room for everything?"

"Tyler will figure it out." Hands at his waist, Gardner glanced back at his brother. "That boy. He knows I fly in supplies. One of these days he'll learn not to drive out without emptying the back of the Rover first."

"You're a good man, Gardner Barnes."

He leaned in exhilaratingly close, his gaze a sizzling blend of everything masculine when he said, "I was good, wasn't I?"

Heart fluttering deliciously at the reminder, Harley pushed against his chest, moving him back—mmmm, eight inches seemed far enough. "I'm not talking about *that* kind of good."

"It's the only kind that counts," he said with a wicked lift of one brow. Capturing her hand, he dragged her palm back and forth across his chest, then urged her fingers lower.

"Would you stop?" She jerked away and could've sworn the tips of her fingers burned. "Someone might see. Besides, I'm trying to give you a compliment."

"You just did."

"Gardner, you are incorrigible. A trait you picked up from your brother no doubt."

Gardner searched Tyler out with stark eyes.

Harley went on. "What I was trying to say is that you and Tyler have a very special relationship. You seem to know when he needs a brother, a father. Or just a friend."

Gardner shrugged and motioned for her to follow around the Rover's front end. He opened the passenger door and handed her in just as Tyler slammed the back. "I've been doing it so long it's second nature. Don't read anything into it."

"Modesty does not become you." Harley put on a schoolteacher scowl.

"It doesn't become you, either, Harley Golden." Hat in one hand, Gardner leaned into the cab, his lips on Harley's ear. "That's why I'm keeping your panties."

Tyler jerked open the driver's door, cutting off Harley's response.

Fist below her chin, Gardner closed her mouth, then reached for the seat belt and fastened her in. His hand barely brushed her lap. Harley felt his touch to the pit of her stomach.

"Give me ten minutes to shut 'er down and I'll be ready to roll. And, Tyler, try to keep it under eighty on the way home."

Gardner slapped the hood of the Rover and trotted back to the plane.

"He's one to talk," Tyler groused, slamming his door. He glanced Harley's way from the corner of one eye. "You ever seen the Roadrunner? You know, the cartoon?"

"A time or two."

"Well, that's Gardner. 'Cept instead of a whirlwind, he whips up an acre of choke-your-mama dust. You can see the ol' boy coming for miles. Gardner screws up shocks like we own Midas."

"Sounds expensive."

Tyler snorted. "Not for Gardner. He's got it made when it comes to slave labor."

It was hard not to grin. "You?"

"Yeah. Me." Tyler cranked up the engine and cut on the AC. "I'm real good at replacing shocks. But then, I'm real good at brake jobs, too."

Harley saw it coming. "The Roadrunner scenario?"

"Gardner runs like the bird, I stop like him," Tyler replied, a wily cant to his mouth. He lifted both brows.

This kid was a heartbreaker. "How long has Gardner been flying?"

"'Bout five years now." Tyler draped his arm across the back of the seat, settling in to tell his story. "He was in Tulsa, ya see, and had what will go down in the Barnes family history as the layover from hell."

"That bad, huh?" Harley barely managed to suppress her smile.

"Seems there were these women romance readers stuck there waiting for the same flight. A couple of 'em tried to talk Gardner into participating in their cover model pageant."

Gardner motioned him forward. Tyler straightened and shifted into gear. "They wouldn't take *no* for an answer, even when Gardner told 'em he didn't believe in love."

Yanking open the back door, Gardner climbed in. Tyler continued. "After that, the ol' boy bought the Cessna. Guess he figures he'd rather risk his life than risk being thought of as a sex object."

Knowing he'd caught the end of Tyler's tale, Harley glanced over her shoulder where Gardner had draped himself over the back seat of the Range Rover.

Tyler chose that moment to floor the gas pedal, tossing Harley against her door. The Rover fishtailed back onto the dirt-and-gravel road. Gardner kicked the back of the seat.

"Sorry 'bout that, Miss Golden."

"No problem." Harley readjusted her seat belt, shot Tyler a quick grin. "I'm a big fan of Saturday-morning cartoons."

"Beep-beep," Tyler said, and floored the pedal again.

"I see it didn't take you two long to get acquainted," Gardner grumbled.

"You know me and the ladies."

Gardner just rolled his eyes. Being the man that he was, letting his speed-happy little brother drive didn't threaten his masculinity. Not that anything could, Harley thought, remembering the way he'd loved her.

Then remembering he didn't believe in love.

Gardner's response to Tyler's commentary on his belief, or lack thereof, was none. Zero. Zilch. No denial. Nothing. It was as if the subject was one he'd learned to tune out, or grown accustomed to ignoring.

The way he ignored his good looks. The way Harley wished she could ignore those extra five pounds on her hips. Irrevocably. And forever. Harley sighed.

While he drove, Tyler talked about his plans for school the following fall, a subject that segued into a dissertation on his true love—veterinary medicine. He described in great and gory detail the horse that had pulled up lame after Gardner's all-night ride. The same horse Gardner had told her about following their first foray into—dare she admit it?—phone sex.

Gardner didn't respond to that line of conversation, either, ignoring, too, the guilt trip his animal-loving brother laid on thick. But beneath every punch Tyler threw, every jab, every barb, he breathed love for his big brother. Gardner had done a father's job well.

Harley wondered if he'd exhausted his parental reserves on Tyler, or if Gardner planned to have children of his own. It would be a lucky woman who shared that with him.

Too bad the man didn't believe in love.

Not that she'd ever truly expected anything permanent out of this . . . this . . . fling. This adventure. Sure, it had been easy to think he could be the man of her dreams when he'd had his hands in places that hadn't been touched by a man in . . . well, in months. A lot of months. Okay, years.

Yes, seeing Gardner, being with Gardner, was taking a risk. But after four years of calcifying along in her nonlife, she wanted to shake off Brad for good.

Who better to help her along in this voyage of self-discovery than one gorgeous cowboy hunk?

The ranch house was exactly what Harley had expected, though she'd had no overt expectations. Wood framed and decades old, the two-story structure looked out over acres and acres of West Texas prairie.

With a covered porch snuggled around three sides, and barn red shutters cuddled up to every window, the house had Home written across each board.

Gardner's home. And Tyler's home. Camelot.

After the roller-coaster ride across the grassland—and a short stop where Gardner introduced her to Excalibur's King of Prince William's Knight—Tyler rolled to an impressively smooth stop behind the house. Giving her a cocky sideways look, he flashed Harley a randy eighteen-year-old smile. Gardner's hand on his shoulder pinned Tyler to the seat.

"Your chauffeuring days are numbered, little brother." Gardner leaned across and snatched the keys from the ignition, then swung open his door. "You'd best stick to doctoring cattle. After you're done with your chores."

Harley pretended not to see Tyler deflate, or hear his grumbled opinion on Gardner's legitimacy. Instead, her gaze followed Gardner as he skirted the front of the vehicle.

Why had she not noticed the way his jeans hugged his buns, the way his thighs flexed taut from a lifetime of gripping horses, the way his belt buckle drew her eyes to . . . Oh, God. What had he done with her panties?

Still mentally searching for her underwear, Harley stepped out when Gardner opened her door. She glanced up, answered his grin with one of her own, then noticed his eyes were not smiling.

Now what was wrong?

"Tyler, go find your uncle," Gardner hollered across the hood at his dour-faced brother. "Tell him we've got company for the rest of the week."

A screen door slammed in answer. "I hear ya, Gardner. I may be about to kick off, but I'm not deaf. And you know as well as I do that the downstairs guest room's just waiting to be used." Jud stopped beside Tyler, propped his hands at his hips and squinted narrow eyes at Gardner. "Your guest got a name?"

Gardner rubbed at his forehead, then made the introductions. "Judson Barnes, this is Harley Golden. Harley, my uncle Jud."

Harley looked from Gardner to Judson to Tyler and wished she could bottle and sell the Barnes male genes. If Gardner was a drop-dead gorgeous hunk—which was a rhetorical comment if she'd ever made one—then Tyler was a teenage heartthrob, and Judson...well, no man should look so good at any age.

Tyler's walnut brown hair was longer than Gardner's, but definitely short. Judson's was longer still, and sprinkled with gray. But all three men had those eyes. Long lashed and nature's green. And their height didn't vary by more than an inch. Eighteen-plus feet of West Texas rancher was an amazing sight.

Harley stepped forward and extended her hand, wondering what other secrets Camelot was keeping to herself. "It's a pleasure, Mr. Barnes. Gardner speaks of you fondly."

"It's good to know he talks about one of us." Jud's scowl was halfhearted. "He hasn't mentioned you at all."

Tyler nudged Jud with his elbow. "I think she's the one from the phone."

"The phone?" This time Jud's frown was legit. "You mean—"

"Yeah," Tyler interrupted. "The phone."

"Ahhh." Judson drew out the sound, then turned and cuffed Tyler on the shoulder. "Then don't stand there gawking, boy. Help your brother with Miss Golden's bags."

He turned back to Harley, his lip curled on one side in a Clint Eastwood grin. Harley decided then and there to find a year-round tanning booth. She needed a good blush defense.

Jud gestured for her to precede him. "Let me show you around the house, Miss Golden. You're just in time for supper."

"Hold on a minute," Gardner barked, shoving Harley's briefcase into Jud's arms and her suitcase into Tyler's. "You two take Harley's things inside and let me have a minute alone with *my* guest."

With a minimum of grumbling and a maximum of speculation, the two men headed for the house.

"You told them about our phone calls," Harley whispered once Jud and Ty were out of earshot.

Gardner shook his head. "Tyler picked up the phone. Once. He didn't hear anything. It's just that my lack of female companionship is a running joke around here."

He lifted his hat, scrubbed one hand over his hair, then settled the wide-brimmed Resistol back in place. "I didn't consider what I was getting you into. I'm sorry."

A man who knew the meaning of the word *sorry*. And even knew how to pronounce it. Just her luck he didn't believe in love. "Is that why you have that wrinkle?"

"What wrinkle?" He frowned.

"This one." She reached up, ran her thumb across his brow. "Don't frown. It makes it worse."

Gardner frowned, making it worse. "I don't have a wrinkle."

"Yes, you do. And you have little lines. Right here." She smoothed a feather-light touch over the corner of his eye, then stroked the spot to the right of his mouth.

"You have a dimple, too. And the longest lashes I've ever seen." She brushed them with a knuckle; his eyes drifted shut. Heat curled between their bodies in corkscrews of summer steam.

"You could use a shave." She cupped his jaw, played his lips with her thumb. "And your mouth tastes like heaven on earth."

"Yours tastes like a cherry. Sweet. Ripe." He palmed the back of her head, brought her flush against his body. He leaned over, sucked her lower lip into his mouth.

Turning his back to the house, he opened her wrap, slid his hand inside to cover her breast. His palm was a fire on her skin, his tongue a flame in her mouth. The kiss skipped straight over seduction and slid into sin. Gardner's sex pumped to life, priming Harley's body with precision skill and speed.

Then he jerked up his head, bit off a curse and set her back a step with regret in his eyes. "Harley, there's a gun under the driver's seat of the Rover. If I come near you again, shoot me. Put me out of my misery."

He did look miserable. A cross between a kid with his hand in Momma's cookie jar and a teen in the back seat of Daddy's Buick. Harley reached out, but pulled back her hand when he flinched.

His misery now looked suspiciously like self-pity. And Harley started to laugh.

Hands jammed at his waist, Gardner gave a disgusted shake of his head and kicked up a spray of gravel dust. "What is so damned funny?"

"This is rich."

"What?"

Harley swiped a thumb pad beneath each eye. "Here you are, you finally have me to yourself—you lecherous ol' man—and we have two chaperons who could do double duty as Catholic school nuns."

"Don't move." Gardner held up one hand. "I'll be right back."

"Where are you going?"

"To get your bags. You haven't unpacked yet. Let's get out of here." He jerked his thumb over his shoulder. "Go back to Fredericksburg."

"You mean back to the fantasy?"

"Right now that's exactly what I want."

"Me, too." And she really did. But she also knew that Fredericksburg had changed everything. "The fantasy's been fun, Gardner, but it can't go on forever. We both need to know where to go from here."

"You're right." Gardner glanced across the yard of Camelot, his eyes narrowed, his expression fierce. Finally, his focus returned to her.

His eyes sparkled, his grin disarmed. "Let's get on with that date. How 'bout some West Texas supper, Harley Golden?"

The man could charm the barbs off a fence. "Thought you'd never ask, cowboy."

8

HARLEY LAID HER FORK on the rim of her plate and smiled across the table at Jud. "Your nephews are lucky men, Mr. Barnes. You're a wonderful cook."

"C'mon now, Miss Golden. I told you to call me Jud. We've got a cash crop of Mr. Barneses populating the place and it'll get mighty confusing if you don't."

"Then Jud it is. As long as you agree to call me Harley." She let her smile widen. It was easy to do.

"Harley." Jud's brows drew together. He waved his knife and fork over his plate. "Ain't that the name of a motorbike?"

Harley nodded. "Harley-Davidson. My parents rode when I was younger."

"Did you ride with them?" Tyler asked, coating his slab of bacon-soaked meat loaf with ketchup.

"I used to. But I haven't been on a bike since I was ten."

"And anything else you two Mr. Barneses want to know will have to wait." Gardner scraped back his chair, got to his feet. "If y'all don't mind, I'd like to show Harley around the ranch before I have to run over to Sam Coltrain's and check on the trailer."

"Hold on a minute, boy," Jud ordered. "Harley hasn't eaten more than half a helping. Why don't you sit back down here and let her finish up?"

Harley stood. "I couldn't eat another bite, Jud. Really. But it was delicious. Can I help you clean up?"

"No, ma'am. This ain't no dude ranch where you gotta work for your supper. And there's no use cleaning up till the rest of the boys eat." Jud pushed back from the table, unfolded his frame from his seat. "Speakin' of which, I'd better holler down to the bunkhouse." He started for the back door, then glanced back at Harley. "As long as you're sure you're finished."

"I'm finished. I can't remember the last time I sat down to a home-cooked meal. I tend to . . . graze. You know, popcorn here, an apple or carrot stick there." Jud stopped walking. Tyler stopped chewing. Gardner stopped to stare. So Harley tried again. "A head of lettuce. A cubic foot of puffed wheat."

No use. All three men still appeared clueless. What did aerobically active ranchers know about cellulite? "It's called low fat, high carbohydrates. I can only do meat loaf in bacon drippings and mashed potatoes with butter once a year. I have a problem with weight."

Now she really felt like a piece of meat. Jud gawked, as if he didn't understand the concept. Tyler understood, but his grin was appreciative, and more leer than grin.

But Gardner. Oh, Gardner. The expression in his eyes defied description. His gaze held a knowledge that came from intimacy, a desire that sprang from the same. The look frightened her, compelled her. She didn't know if she could live up to what he expected.

Her blood heated; her stomach knotted. She was totally, irrevocably lost. "So how about that tour you promised?"

He must've read the panic in her eyes because he skirted the table and took her elbow in his hand. "Are you sure you're up to it? It's quite a climb to the attic."

Standing in the doorway between the washroom and the back porch, Jud sputtered. "The attic? I done showed Harley the house, Gardner. Why don't you walk her around the homestead? There's nothing in the attic but a bunch of old junk."

"Harley's an antique dealer, Jud. She appreciates all that *junk*."

The inflection Gardner gave the word *junk* told Harley that Gardner and his uncle held differing opinions on whatever was stored in the attic. She couldn't wait to find out what it was. And what it meant to Gardner.

Before Gardner managed to move toward the doorway that led to the stairs, Jud nodded in his direction. "So I guess you'll be wanting off breakfast duty this week."

Gardner pulled up short at Jud's question. His hand tightened noticeably on Harley's arm. Harley glanced up at his face—at his drawn expression, the tightness around his mouth.

"Like you said, Jud. This isn't a dude ranch. I'll take care of my chores. Harley knows the lay of the land— that Camelot comes first."

So much for worship and adoration.

Jud afforded Gardner a stern fatherly look. "I wasn't expecting you to dodge your duties, Gardner. But I thought by taking breakfast off your hands, I could free you up a couple of hours to spend with your guest."

Tyler rose, carried his plate to the sink. "And unless you've got your heart set on going out to Sam Coltrain's tonight, I can save you the trip. I've gotta pick up Guin from Doc Harmon's after school tomorrow, anyway. I'll run over to Sam's and pick up the trailer."

"It's ready?"

"He called while you were gone." Tyler dried his mouth on a dish towel. "Said the weld's not pretty, but it oughtta hold up to whatever King gives it."

Harley glanced from Gardner's face to the two men standing, arms crossed, on either side of the kitchen sink. The scene resembled a hostile standoff. But the emotion in Jud's eyes wasn't criticism but concern, the care in Ty's gaze the same.

Gardner crossed the width of the kitchen, reached out and shook each man's hand. "You two aren't half-bad to have around."

"We're all Barneses," Tyler said. "What did you expect?"

With a final slap to both men's shoulders, Gardner turned away. There was a story here. Harley wondered what it was. But before she could wonder further, Gardner laced his fingers through hers and led her up the stairs with a minimum of ceremony and a whole lot of haste.

The landing at the top of the stairs branched off to the right into a hallway that ran the width of the house. Jud had showed her the bedrooms—his own, Gardner's and Ty's—before showing her the room in which she'd be staying. Downstairs.

On this leg of the tour, as in the first, she had the opportunity to sneak nothing but a quick peek into Gardner's room. It wasn't enough. She wanted to see more.

She wanted to see if he made his bed, if he hung up his clothes, if the room smelled of Gardner. She wanted to see where she wouldn't be sleeping. But she walked on by because he waited at the end of the hall, his hand on the knob of the only door Jud had not opened earlier.

She flattened her hand, shoulder high, on the glossy white wood. "What just happened downstairs?"

"Supper. The traditional meal families eat together at the end of the day."

"I know what supper is."

"Funny. I didn't get that impression from what you said."

"What I said is that I don't sit down to many home-cooked meals."

"That's right. You don't cook. You don't even eat. You graze." Arms crossed over his chest, Gardner leaned back against the door. "Animals graze, Harley."

His statement said more than three words should. Uh-oh. Looked as if the after-sex euphoria was over. "C'mon, Gardner. I don't mean that I stand in a field and eat hay."

"Then tell me exactly what it is you mean."

"I eat when I'm hungry, not when the hour of the day demands. If I get busy with book work, or spend a long day on the phone tracking down a particular item, I may not eat for hours."

He didn't look convinced, or satisfied, so she tried again.

"I don't rope dogies, or wrestle steers, or whatever ranchers do all day. I function best by eating light, not to mention that with my metabolism I can't eat any differently without gaining weight."

She gave up then, because Gardner's frown told her she'd dug herself in deeper.

"Well, then, it's a good thing that you don't have a family." He opened the door and stepped through.

"What's that supposed to mean?"

He stopped and turned to the side, his face no less handsome for the turmoil the shadowed attic stairway couldn't hide. "Growing kids can't do much with puffed wheat and popcorn."

With that, and a punctuating shrug, he took the stairs two at a time. His heavy steps stomped out any hope Harley had at keeping this conversation light.

So typical. Just like a man to walk away with the last word. And wrong word at that.

"Wait a minute, Gardner." Harley hitched up her skirt and trudged up the narrow staircase into the center of the huge, slant-ceilinged attic. Broad shafts of sunlight streamed in through the four dormer windows spaced along the front wall of the house.

The light wasn't bright enough to illuminate every corner. But it was enough. She was dying to explore. And she would. Later.

Gardner stood gazing out the farthest window, his profile rigid, his expression harsh. She didn't know how she'd disappointed him, but she intended to find out. Because three hours ago, with both body and soul, she'd made a commitment. A commitment she was determined to see through.

"I'm lost here, Gardner." The floorboards creaked like old bones beneath her boots. She laid her hand on Gardner's wrist. "It happened somewhere between the mashed potatoes and the puffed wheat, but I really don't think it had anything to do with food."

His mouth quirked. It wasn't a real smile, but it gave Harley hope. "C'mon, cowboy. Spill the beans."

"Sounds like food to me," he said, and this time she caught a glimpse of his dimple.

"Ahhh. He speaks. But does he talk?"

"I know how to talk." With his free hand, he covered her fingers where she still held his wrist. Slow and seeking, his gaze moved over her face. "Don't tell me you've forgotten those phone calls."

He mesmerized her. Though the beams of light left his face slightly shadowed, the depth of emotion dark in his eyes threatened to throw her off track.

She lifted his hand, kissed the tip of one finger, then closed her eyes and shuddered at the feel of his thumb shamelessly teasing her mouth. "You're trying to change the subject."

"Is it working?" He breathed the question against her cheek, then touched his tongue to her lips.

Yes. "No."

"How 'bout if I try this?"

He held both her wrists in one of his hands. The fingers of the other made for a persuasive argument, but she would stay strong.

She put only enough space between them to distract him, not dissuade him. "That's enough."

He nuzzled her neck. "Are you sure?"

"Yes." For now.

He'd reached her ear, and his tongue . . . ahh.

"How long until now is over?" he asked.

"Until you tell me your secrets."

"How do I know I can trust you?"

If he didn't know by now . . . "You think I'd reveal the intimate details of a man who still has my panties?"

At that, Gardner chuckled and let her go. Harley wrapped herself in relief, and then in the crook of Gardner's elbow. She snuggled close to his side, remembering his smell, how nice he felt, how incredibly warm and safe and comfortable he made her feel.

He held her like nothing else mattered, then pulled her in front of him and snugged his arm around her waist. She tucked her head beneath his chin; her eyes followed the direction of his gaze. Together they stared out the window, across miles of prairie, acres of productive land, over a grazing herd of cattle and an endless expanse of blue-white sky.

This land would be easy to love. And equally demanding of anyone willing to give up so much of their time, their life. The sacrifice would take a special kind of man.

The man holding her. The man whose sigh was not only a breath, but a letting go of pent-up thoughts. Harley braced herself for his confrontation—a confrontation she'd asked for.

"Downstairs," Gardner began, "you told Tyler that you hadn't been on the back of a bike since you were ten. Did you ride with your parents?"

"Everly and I both did," she replied. Though she wasn't sure exactly what he wanted to know, she hadn't a doubt of his question's importance. And Gardner Barnes was worth a bumpy trip down memory lane. "Once we were old enough, we both preferred not to go along. Buck and Trixie didn't seem to mind."

"Buck and Trixie?"

"Pretty bad, huh."

He let that sink in, then said, "So you were ten."

Harley thought a minute. "Actually, the first time they let us stay home I was about seven."

"Seven?" His arms around her waist tightened. "How old was Everly?"

"Nine going on thirty." Already, she knew what he was thinking. "We were both pretty old for being so young. Definitely not your typical kids."

Gardner released her and Harley turned. Shaking his head, he walked to a far corner of the attic and propped his boot on the torn red vinyl of an old kitchen chair beside a brass-bound trunk.

The business side of Harley's mind immediately estimated the worth of the piece. And of the oak armoire standing behind. Impressive. But her emotional side saw nothing but Gardner's unrest.

His elbow braced on his knee, he leaned forward and wiped a smudge off one corner of the trunk. "What kind of parents would go off and leave a seven- and nine-year-old home alone?"

"It wasn't for long periods of time, Gardner. Usually just a few hours on Sunday," Harley answered, staying where she was. The sunlight warmed the space where Gardner had left her standing.

"Usually?"

"Once in a while they went on a weekend ride. But Everly and I did fine." She began to pace, noting the lack of dust, the absence of a musty smell. Even the windows had the type of clean shine that hers at home rarely saw.

This room was used for more than storage. Someone came up here often. She thought she knew who. "You've got to understand, Gardner. Our parents were kids themselves when Everly and I were born. I'm sure they thought of us as playthings instead of a responsibility. But we turned out okay."

"No thanks to them."

She made her way around the trunk and fingered the latch on the armoire. "I don't know. They taught me a lot about parenting."

"Nice trick, considering they didn't…" Gardner gave a sound of disgust.

Her fist locked around the pull of the armoire's door. She shook her head, dazed and frowning, thrown and out of sync. Her parents hadn't loved her. Was that what he'd stopped himself from saying?

Five simple words. Words she'd never wanted to believe.

Her parents hadn't loved her. Knowing Gardner believed those words gave truth to that ugly fact.

Releasing the handle, she glanced down at the red crescent imprinted on her palm. "What I learned, Gardner, was that an innocent child needs parents who have the time and energy to handle that kind of responsibility. I don't. So I've chosen not to have a family."

Gardner stiffened and brought his boot down hard on the floor. She'd hit a nerve. No. The chord she'd struck ran deeper, its source a belief as deeply ingrained as his love for the land.

Oh, yes, she'd seen the way he'd looked when they'd flown over Camelot. It was a look he should have worn for a woman. A look she wanted him to wear when he thought of her. It went beyond that first rush of love into contentment and security for life.

She remembered then that he'd told her he wanted a family. Children to whom he'd leave this inheritance. Is that why he'd invited her here? Was this an interview? A satisfaction-guaranteed-or-your-money-back-no-risk-trial-period?

She turned around and, arms crossed, lifted her chin. The trunk stood between them like a line in the sand. "Okay, Gardner. Ask me anything you want."

He frowned. "I don't have anything to ask you."

"Yes, you do. That's why you brought me here. To see if I'd meet your qualifications for motherhood." She arched one brow, daring him to deny the charge.

His eyes glittered but he didn't look away. "I meant it as a compliment, not an insult."

"A compliment?" Harley shoved tense hands through her hair, then fluffed the locks with an exasperated shake of her head. "The way the three of you were looking at me downstairs I felt like a prospective brood mare."

"You're a beautiful, passionate woman, Harley Golden." His gaze lingered intimately, then lingered still. "A man would be lucky to have you bear his children."

Harley closed her eyes. He found her beautiful, he found her passionate, but he said not a word about love.

Well, this was the make-or-break point with her. Looking up slowly, she said, "Children or not, a man would be lucky to have me. Period."

Gardner met her obstinate gaze head-on. "I didn't say he wouldn't."

"No, but it wasn't the first thought that crossed your mind." She waited a minute, gathering her thoughts, searching for the words to make him understand.

"I've been through one marriage where my husband expected me to understand that because of career demands he had only two evenings a week to spend with me." Her mouth twisted into a wry grimace. "Of course, I didn't know until it was too late how he spent the other five."

"You shouldn't have had to go through that."

"No, I shouldn't have. But it happened. And I won't plead selfish for demanding any future relationship be on my own terms."

Gardner settled his hands at his hips. "Which means no children."

"It's not the contradiction it sounds like, Gardner. A child deserves more time and attention than my life-style affords. A child needs a better start in life than having a parent who's too busy to be there for flying kites and long division."

How could she make him understand? How could she tell him what it had been like? She and Gardner didn't have a future unless she could get him to see things her way.

UNLESS HE COULD get her to see things his way, he and Harley didn't have a future.

She didn't plan to have children. Not that she never would, but she had no plans. The distinction left room for discussion. And Gardner hadn't made it this far without learning the art of persuasion.

"What if you changed your life-style?"

"What would that solve? I'm happy doing what I do. I'm *good* at what I do." Gesturing with her hands, she began to pace the four feet of floor running lengthwise between the trunk and the armoire. "If I make a change and I'm unhappy, I don't think I would be the best mother I could be. And that wouldn't be fair to my children."

Gardner spun the chair around and straddled it backward, placing himself at one end of Harley's path. "What if you didn't have to work at all?"

Stopping mid-step, Harley slowly turned around. "If I had a husband to keep me in the manner to which I deserve to become accustomed?"

He didn't even try to stop the smile tilting the corner of his mouth. "Something like that."

"I don't know, Gardner."

"Being a mother wouldn't make you happy?"

"You mean, would I be content to be a wife and mother? You mean, do I have to have a career?" She resumed her restless movements, walking out into the center of the room.

Gardner shifted forward in the chair. This looked as if it might take a while.

"No, I don't have to have a career. I could turn antiquing into a hobby. Or a second income." She fingered the gold inlay on a hat-and-umbrella stand. "But I'd only do that under one condition. And it's a condition I've set on any relationship, whether I'm a working woman or a stay-at-home mom.

"I want a man who will love me more than anything else. More than his job, our children, or even the land."

A weighty silence settled between them. The beams of sunlight seemed to dim. Gardner watched the shadows fall. "You don't want much, do you?"

"I want everything." Her words were crisp, clean, and cutting.

He felt the blade go deep. "I want to show you something."

Unlatching the trunk, Gardner leaned forward and lifted the lid. He was determined to make Harley understand the importance of his family.

"My great-grandfather was a rural doctor. The only one in this area for miles. He and my great-grandmother married back East. He'd gone to the same school his father attended and was expected to follow in the family footsteps.

"Both my great-grandparents came from well-to-do families, and both wanted to start family traditions of their own. Their parents weren't thrilled. But they came here, anyway. With virtually nothing to their names. The only things of value they owned were the French lace on my great-grandmother's wedding gown and my great-grandfather's medical kit.

"I keep them both in here." Gardner removed a faded patchwork quilt from the top of the trunk and draped it over the upraised lid. He motioned Harley to step around.

"My grandfather wanted to be a doctor, too. His father taught him a lot but couldn't afford to send him to school.

"So my grandfather started the ranch, and from stories my father used to tell I gather the only medicine he practiced was on his own animals."

"Maybe that's where Tyler gets his interest."

"Maybe. Ranching and doctoring run in Barnes blood. But it is blood, Harley. Family. Camelot is more than tradition. It's a legacy with a history that ties it back through generations."

Harley ran her fingertips along the surface of the quilt. "It's a history to be proud of."

"Proud is only a part of it. It's also a tradition I *will* carry on." He stood then, holding his ground, reinforcing the stand he'd taken when his father had chosen death over his sons. "The land is always there, Harley. It doesn't make cheap promises. It doesn't lie."

Harley raised her chin. "And it doesn't love you."

"I don't believe in love." He refolded the quilt and slammed the lid of the trunk.

Her eyes glinted and, as Gardner watched, awareness replaced puzzlement. She shoved a lock of hair behind her ear. "Then what happened this afternoon?"

Gardner felt like a ton of bull had just kicked his insides out. He knew how uncertain she'd been today when they'd spent those hours making lo . . . in bed.

"Gardner," Tyler called from the bottom of the stairs. "The foreman out at Acre 52's on the phone. Something about a drill bit."

Gardner didn't move.

Arms crossed defiantly over her chest, Harley took a deep breath, lifted her chin and met his gaze. "You'd better go."

He still didn't move. He needed to explain. To tell her about his parents, his father, and why he didn't believe in love.

"Gardner!" Tyler yelled.

"Go," Harley urged, tilting her head toward the stairs.

Hands braced low on his hips, he said, "We're not through here."

"I think you've said enough."

Frustration ground through him. "Don't jump to conclusions about this afternoon, Harley."

"What about this afternoon?" she asked, her eyebrows lifted in innocence.

"Gardner!"

"I'm coming," he yelled down at Tyler. "Look, Harley—"

"Go take your phone call, Gardner. Camelot comes first, remember?" The twist of her lips wasn't a smile at all. "I know the lay of the land."

Knowing he had to go didn't ease the struggle between his head and heart. He turned for the stairs, leaving Harley behind. And each descending step felt like one headed in the wrong direction.

9

HARLEY LAY DOWNSTAIRS in the king-size guest bed listening to the house settle in for the night. The curtains hanging on the window above the bed remained open.

Moonlight spilled across the rough-beamed ceiling, casting a warped tic-tac-toe shadow on the white stucco wall. The floorboard above the ceiling creaked. That should be Tyler, she thought, mentally retracing the steps of her tour.

Water ran through ancient pipes, but the ping and clang of expanding copper pipes was farther down the hall. More an echo than straight overhead. She guessed the source of the sound to be Gardner's bath.

She turned to her side and punched up her pillow, then mashed a depression the size of Gardner's hard head in the center of the second pillow's case. So much for honesty. And so much for spending her time off with Gardner.

She'd told him how she felt and now here she lay. Alone.

Not that he'd said he wouldn't join her, but she didn't think he would. Making love would only be a bandage on the problems they'd left unresolved. Their differences were not insurmountable. If a woman could climb Mount Everest, well . . .

The attic session was worthy of a confessional, or a psychiatrist's couch. While hurtful memories had made Gardner reject love, they'd deepened her need for the same. She'd dredged up a lot of past angst and two of the major reasons for her conviction. Her parents and Brad.

Each had offered casual attention and affection—fine if she'd been the family dog. But her psyche demanded more. She wanted love. And she wanted it from Gardner Barnes, because in him she saw such promise, a chance at the relationship she'd wanted all her life.

If only she could convince him that the love he said he didn't believe in was an inherent part of the man he was. She'd seen it in his dealings with Tyler and Jud, and felt it in his heartbeat, in his very breath, while lying close in his arms.

Yeah, but you're forgetting something really big here, Harley. The man wants children and you don't.

And even as she thought it, she knew it was a lie.

She wanted to scream her lungs out at that first Little League win, hold her breath those first few yards without training wheels, stay up till midnight and hear all about that first date.

She wanted Gardner Barnes to be her children's father.

It had taken the finding of the man she wanted, the man she truly loved, to resurrect the dream. The career options she'd laid out earlier would incorporate easily into a mother's life. And she wouldn't have to worry about parenting alone—not with the importance Gardner placed on family. She had no doubt he would be as involved as a father could be.

Only one minor obstacle remained. Gardner's closed heart. The attention and worship she was flexible on. And she was more than willing to make the necessary career adjustments. But her insistence on pure and perfect love, for herself and her children, was nonnegotiable.

The phone on her night table shrilled. She grabbed it up without hesitation. "Gardner?"

He chuckled, a resonant rumble that warmed her skin like winter's first fire. God, she'd grown to love that laugh.

"I was thinking you might not answer." But he sounded glad that she had.

"Habit, I guess. I didn't stop to think where I was." Ha! And if he believed that, she had a couple of oil wells . . .

"No, I mean, I didn't know if you would want to talk to me."

Men. Go figure. "When have I ever not wanted to talk to you?"

"How about two hours ago in the attic?"

"Oh, yeah. Then." Tyler's interruption had put their conversation on hold, though it was by no means finished. Neither was it a discussion she wanted to continue on the phone. "Where are you?"

"'Bout a mile from the house."

"I thought I just heard you upstairs."

"Must've been Jud. He was afraid he'd disturb you if he used the bath at the head of the stairs. I told him to clean up in mine." The connection buzzed, then cleared. "Uh, Harley?"

"Hmmm?"

"If you thought you heard me upstairs, that means you *were* thinking about where you are."

Ooops. Caught in a web of her own deceit. "Yeah, I guess I was."

"You guess?"

"Okay. So I was." But no way would she tell him she'd been wishing he was with her.

"Do you want me there with you?"

Now he was telepathic. "What happens if I say no?"

"Then that's the end of it."

The end of what? This phone call? Her time on the ranch? The chance to show this man what he was missing? "And what if I say yes?"

"Why don't you say it and find out?"

She wanted to. She really wanted to. "I don't think the nuns would approve."

"What the nuns don't know..." His comment dragged suggestively.

Harley curled her toes deep into snowy sheets. "C'mon, Gardner. How can they not know?"

"You're right." That wicked chuckle came again. "You do know how to make some noise."

"Gardner," she moaned, thankful that he couldn't see her face, then wondering why it mattered. He'd seen everything else.

"Embarrassed, Harley?"

Whipping up the covers, she ducked under, phone and all. The close quarters only amplified her groan.

Gardner laughed out loud. "Harley Golden, you are one funny lady."

She pouted for effect, then remembered he couldn't see. "Funny ha-ha? Or funny strange?"

"After all we've done with each other, all we've said, I can't believe you're embarrassed by those lusty little sounds that purr up your throat."

The flame on her face burned its way down her chest. "You're not exactly the strong silent type yourself, Gardner Barnes."

He snorted. "I'll give you the silent. But I think I showed considerable strength resisting you as long as I did."

Feeling a touch of triumph, Harley eased from beneath the covers. "Such willpower. I think a whole sixty minutes elapsed from the first time I saw you until we were in bed."

"What can I say? I'm a sucker for a woman in white panties."

Harley cringed. "Uh, Gardner, about those panties . . ."

A victorious laugh echoed down the line. "Don't even think you're going to get them back."

What did he expect her to say to that? "You said you're about a mile from the house?"

"Yeah, sitting in the Rover with the door wide open. I finished up with the foreman at Acre 52 and ran over a buried gate hinge on the way back. I had to stop and change the tire and, well . . . this is my favorite spot on the ranch. I haven't been out here in a while."

The Rover's door slammed, and Harley heard the give-and-take of metal. "Are you on your way back?"

"Not yet. I'm standing outside, leaning against the fender, enjoying the view. There's a pecan tree here whose limbs spread out over a stock pond. And right now there's at least a million stars twinkling off the water's surface."

Harley closed her eyes and joined him. The blue velvet sky appeared overhead; stars sifted like fairy dust behind her closed lids. The cane blades of the ceiling fan ruffled air through her hair, and stirred up the scent of outdoors.

Gardner cleared his throat. "One day, Harley, I'm going to bring my kids here. I want them to climb this tree and look out over this land. Their land. Land that stretches forever. I want them to see a sky that touches the ground.

"I want them to hear the night. The crickets and frogs at the edge of the pond. The splash of a crappie feeding on bugs. Cattle when they drink. Coyotes from miles away. The wind."

Harley heard it all, and more. Gardner's voice was resonant with awe and respect and love for the land he called home, and Harley reinforced her determination to discover the reason he thought he couldn't give a woman the same.

"Sounds like heaven. I'd love to see it."

"I tell you what." Metal creaked and the phone line whined, then silenced. "Looks like I'll have some free time Friday thanks to Tyler and Jud. We can pack a picnic supper and I'll show you the Barneses' concept of camping out."

"Our second date?"

"A date. A seduction. An assignation. Call it whatever you want. Just don't be surprised when I skip the main course and go straight for dessert."

She remembered him naked, remembered him inside her, and decided she'd starve before Friday arrived.

"I don't know if I can wait three days." He echoed her sentiment with low-spoken words.

"Neither do I," she admitted, feeling light-headed already.

"Do you know why I'm not with you right now?"

"I've got a good idea."

"Then you agree that we both have a lot of thinking to do after today?"

Nodding, Harley sighed, knowing it would be a miracle if they solved anything before Friday. "Thinking is all I've been doing since I got into bed."

"I've been thinking about that. You. In bed. Or rather, you and me in bed this afternoon. About how you'd look pregnant with my child."

"Gardner—"

"I know. You don't want kids." Already husky, his voice dropped to an even lower pitch. "When I have children—and I will have them, Harley—there'll never be a doubt in their mind that they're wanted. I'll be there for them twenty-four hours a day."

A brick wall couldn't have hit her any harder. Why was he twisting her words? Why was he turning on her this way? Why now?

Gardner went on. "There won't be any weekend road trips where they stay at home alone. And they'll never climb in bed at night and wonder why I haven't talked to them all day."

Oh, God. He wasn't only talking about her past. He was talking about his own, as well. And he'd just boiled down their conflict to the reason she wouldn't bring children into a home without love.

"I have no doubt that you'll want them. But will you love them?" Taking a deep breath, Harley forged ahead.

"Will you be annoyed by those midnight calls for a glass of water? The bedsheets that have to be changed hours later? Will you resent spending your night nursing a fever when you need your sleep for a meeting the next day?

"Those things require love, Gardner. I should know. Everly loved me enough to do them for me when Buck and Trixie didn't have the time."

When he didn't say anything she wondered if she'd gone too far. She heard a heavy sigh and then, "Do one thing for me, Harley."

His voice was gruff and it gave her pause.

"If I can."

"If anything happens because of this afternoon, you let me know."

Harley pressed her hand low on her belly. "Nothing's going to happen, Gardner."

"Condoms aren't one hundred percent effective, Harley. We both know that," he said, then released a long audible breath.

"What's wrong, Gardner?"

"Nothing. Nothing at all."

"Then what is it?"

"God, Harley," he groaned. "I can't imagine anything more beautiful than one of your babies. Except for you."

Harley closed her eyes and let the thrill of his words give her hope. The beauty he referred to was not of the flesh, but of the kind they'd created together in bed. She had to believe that. Her hope started there, knowing that Gardner was a man with deep feelings.

And by damn, she'd convince him he could extend those feelings to love.

"Well," she began, her voice hoarse, her concentration thrown. "I think you're beautiful, too."

He gave a short laugh. "C'mon, Harley. A man? Beautiful?"

"Yes. Beautiful. And caring." Time to inject a new mood. She purposefully lightened her voice. "Granted, a little gruff, but it's nothing we can't work on."

"We?"

"Yeah, we." This time her smile was true. "I'm not going anywhere until I get my picnic . . . and my panties."

STANDING IN HIS stocking feet, Gardner leaned over to stare into the refrigerator, one arm propped on the open door. The house had been quiet when he'd come in but he'd still left his boots in the washroom.

Jud had been trying to whip Gardner into proper husband material ever since he'd brought Harley home. Leaving mud tracked across the kitchen wouldn't do. Neither would working until 11:00 p.m.

What should have been another short trip to the drilling site had turned into three hours. Not that he didn't trust the crew to handle emergencies. He did. And he'd hated going off and leaving Harley after supper again.

But if he didn't keep his finger on the pulse of Camelot's operations, he'd lose everything he'd worked for his entire life.

The crude oil wells didn't provide the income they once had, but a dollar was a dollar. Beef prices fluctuated, as did the profit from the acreage he occasionally leased. So far, King's stud fees seemed to be generating a steady income, but there was no guarantee for the future.

Gardner put in whatever time he had to. Because making every dollar, every hour, every venture, count had gotten him where he was today.

And as much as he wanted Harley, once he'd gotten her on the ranch, things changed. He'd seen how easily she'd become a distraction, how he'd wanted to spend time with her instead of on business. Staying out until eleven the past two nights hadn't been easy. But it had been necessary.

He'd worked eight years to undo the damage his father's negligence had caused the family business, the damage it had done to his sons. Gardner wouldn't let an emotion as controlling, as destructive, hell, as abused and distorted, as love wreck what he'd built out of Camelot, for his family, or for himself.

Just about the same time he realized the refrigerator held no answers and he wasn't hungry, anyway, he heard a squeal of delight and a loud yell of "Checkmate" from the den. He padded down the hallway and stopped.

Jud sat forward in his recliner, his chess set open on the coffee table squared in front of his chair. Harley sat opposite him on the floor, her legs curled to her side, her hair a halo in the low lamplight.

Her exultant smile lit her eyes and she threw her head back and laughed. "I can't believe it. I won. I actually won."

Gardner didn't hear his uncle's reply. He was too busy staring at Harley. He started to retreat, head back through the kitchen to the washroom, grab his boots, shove his feet deep inside and spend the night on the prairie. Or at the drilling site. Or at the two-bit motel in town.

But as if she sensed him standing there, Harley turned. And no matter how badly he needed to move, he couldn't.

She was glad to see him. More than glad. Her face was brighter than sunshine, her eyes telling him she'd been waiting for him to come home. He wanted nothing more than to cross the room, scoop her into his arms, carry her up to his bed and let her soothe his aches and pains.

Instead, he walked into the den and collapsed on the far end of the couch.

"Can you believe it, Gardner?" Harley asked. "I finally won over this wily old uncle of yours."

From the dazed look in his uncle's eyes, Gardner knew it to be true. Jud hadn't let her win. She'd done it. And no doubt earned herself a place of honor in the old man's heart.

"So, Jud, how much did you lose?" Gardner flung one arm along the back of the couch and stretched his legs out wide.

"It's the damnedest thing I ever saw." Jud shook his head and looked up. "And I didn't lose anything but a couple of hours' sleep."

"How's that?" Gardner asked.

"Harley had agreed to do breakfast if she lost this round."

"And now I get to sleep in," Harley said, grinning. "I like my eggs over easy, if you don't mind."

"After a game like that you deserve to have them delivered to your room," Jud said, getting to his feet and patting Harley's shoulder as he passed. "Your turn, Gardner. See if you can salvage the Barnes reputation."

"Not tonight."

"Can't stand the thought of losing?" Harley asked, swinging around on her knees to face him. Her face was alive with playful traces of the girl he'd imagined making cutout cookies. Yet the next minute all he saw was the woman to whom he'd made love.

He had to be careful or the combination would be his undoing.

He shook his head. "Can't find the strength to even think."

"Well, I'm off to bed." Jud headed out of the room, stopping once at the door. "But don't think I'll forget our date," he said to Harley. "I'll be expecting you about seven."

"Ugh. Don't remind me," she groaned.

Once Jud was gone, Gardner settled deeper into the couch cushions. "What was that all about?"

"I lost the first game." She crinkled her nose. "I have to do the breakfast dishes."

"I told you I didn't want you working while you were here," Gardner said.

"Ease up, Gardner," Harley replied, storing the chess set under Jud's lamp table. "I need something to do to keep me busy."

Damn it, she was right. Keeping his distance was no way to treat a guest. He was tired of the distance, tired of the fight within himself. Tired of his father's mistakes ruling his life.

He spread his legs wider, pulled his shirt from his jeans and popped the first button on his fly. "Why don't you crawl up here in my lap and let me keep you busy?"

She pushed the coffee table back into place and stood. Arms crossed, she pointedly frowned at his erection. "I'm not sure this is the time or place for your idea of busy."

Gardner rolled his eyes. "Harley, I'm tired. I've been in these clothes for eighteen hours. I've got grit and sweat in places I don't want to think about." He pressed his hand to the rise of his fly. "That's not going to stop me from getting hard and wanting you more than I want to breathe.

"But right now all I want is for you to climb up here, settle your bottom on my lap and kiss me until neither one of us can see straight. I'm too exhausted to manage anything else. And if that's too much to ask, I'll settle for a good-night hug."

He'd barely managed to open his arms before she'd snuggled deep into his body. He wrapped his arms around her and hugged them both, wondering when anything had ever felt so perfect in his life, wondering how he was going to manage once she went home.

Long minutes later, Harley looked up. She smoothed her thumb over the corners of his eyes. "You look tired."

Gardner dropped his head back against the couch. "I am tired. And dirty. And I no doubt reek."

She buried her face in his chest and inhaled. "You smell like hard honest work."

"And grease and oil and sweat. Not exactly *GQ*-scented material."

"Mmmm. Much better." She cuddled closer, drawing her entire body onto his and tucking her feet between his legs.

"I could get used to this," he murmured, his eyes drifting shut as Harley's weight settled so comfortably against him.

"How about this?" she asked, the fingers of one hand pressing hard at his nape, circling over and over against the tight knots of muscle.

"Yeah, that, too," he managed, sinking deeper into oblivion. Her other hand took up the same motion, running a line from his biceps over his shoulder and up to his neck. She pressed, massaged, rubbed, and squeezed. And Gardner groaned.

"Feel good?"

"You have to ask?" He moaned again. Ecstasy.

"You ought to hire a masseuse," Harley whispered, dusting tiny kisses along his jaw.

"No way." His body was gelatin.

"Why not? You need it. You're enjoying it. It's obviously doing you good."

"You're doing me good." The hand at his nape was now at his scalp. His head bounced twice as his chin hit his chest.

"A professional would know which muscles need the kinks worked out."

I'll show you kinks, he thought, then said, "I don't want a professional. I want you."

She leaned forward, still rubbing, still massaging, and flicked her tongue against his ear. "Why?"

"Why what?" He was hot. Liquid. Burning up and melting at the same time.

"Why do you want me?"

"I'm too tired to think, Harley. And I'm way too tired to talk."

"I don't want you to talk, Gardner. And I don't want you to think." Leaning back against the couch arm, she pulled his head to her chest and tucked him close. "I want you to feel. Just close your eyes and feel."

How could he help but feel with the way she touched him? The way she pulled exhaustion from his body and eased him into the hazy edges of sleep. The way she rocked his body with hers, holding him until he slumbered beneath her.

The way she punched holes in the logical way he'd planned out his life.

That wasn't supposed to have happened, he thought, then Harley turned out the lights.

FRIDAY MORNING, when Harley woke, she was alone on the couch in the den. Gardner's warmth and smell were the only things left of the hours she'd spent curled into his side, legs and arms tangled, fingers and lips never far from bare patches of skin.

She stretched, smiled and decided she could easily grow used to such nights. Then she decided those long days spent learning chess from Everly were worth every minute. If not for winning that second game from Jud, she'd have lost out on precious time with Gardner.

Whether or not she'd made any progress last night remained to be seen. She'd shown him gentle love, soothing love, love born of care and compassion. Today was their picnic, tonight their camp-out, and she planned to show him more.

She didn't even mind the prospect of dishes this morning, though when she got to the kitchen—after a quick detour to her room for a shower and change of clothes—she found the drainer full and the dishwasher running.

Not only had Jud cleaned the kitchen, he'd left her a plate of biscuits and ham and had written out instructions on reheating the gravy in the microwave. She chuckled to herself after reading his note, and decided he didn't understand that cooking for one had taught her the finer points of the digital meal.

Even though she could well afford to skip breakfast—especially after Tuesday night's meat loaf, Wednesday night's chicken-fried steak and Thursday night's pork chops—she sat down at the table and ate. The clock above the humming refrigerator ticked its way to eight. The silence was more than Harley could stand.

Starting the past two days at 5:30 a.m. with a rowdy bunch of cowboys was an experience not to be missed. And she missed it. Strange that, for someone who'd never been a morning person, she hadn't had a bit of trouble making it to the kitchen in time to share the first meal of the day with this overgrown family of men.

Gardner had told her about Judson and Ty, but he'd failed to mention Ol' Pete, or the seven other wranglers living on Camelot that made up the Barneses' extended family. And what a family it was. Food fights at the breakfast table. Tall tales stacked one on top of the other. Discussions of the day ahead and who might need help with what.

Sure they were trying to impress her. She was a guest. But it didn't lessen the attention they paid to one another. She was so glad Gardner had brought her home. She couldn't imagine a finer place to raise a child.

After cleaning her dishes, she headed outside, stopping on the back porch to take in the view. The screen door bounced once and smacked her on the rear, sending her down the steps with a smile.

Half the dry dusty yard had settled into the leather creases of her red ropers by the time she reached the scattered outbuildings. Next to what looked to be a mechanic's shed, she found the lower half of Jud sticking out from beneath the Range Rover. The words she heard from his upper half dissuaded her from saying hello. She'd thank him for doing the dishes later.

Continuing on, she stepped inside the barn. The shadows were cool, ripe with the smell of hay and grain, worn leather and animal musk. Tiny coos and murmurs issued from beyond the long row of stalls. She headed in that direction, realizing the voice was Tyler's. When the mutterings became words and the words took on meaning, she stopped.

"C'mon, now. Quit your beggin'. Man, you women are all alike. You gotta be waited on hand and foot."

Brow furrowed, Harley stepped closer. There was something compelling about Tyler's tone—and the distinctly canine sound of the whimpers that had now reached her ears.

"C'mon, Guin. I'm not asking for a lot. Look, you can ignore your old man but you can't ignore your doctor. Now open your mouth."

Harley stopped at the last stall. The dog lying on a pallet of old quilts and blankets had long since caught her scent and was obviously ignoring Tyler and the pill he held in favor of this newest distraction.

Tyler shushed the weak bark and looked up from where he'd hunkered down next to the dog. "Hey."

"Hey, yourself," Harley responded, making her way cautiously into the stall.

"Gardner's not here."

"I didn't think he would be." Slowly, so as not to alarm the dog, Harley maneuvered into a sitting position. She leaned back against the plank wall and drew her knees to her chest. "The house was too quiet. I saw Jud under the Rover, but I don't think he's in the mood for company."

"Well, company's definitely welcome in here," Tyler said, scratching a spot behind the dog's left ear. "I'm surprised Guinevere's pitiful pleas for attention haven't brought the entire crew running."

"What happened?" Harley asked, noting the bandage circling the black, brown and white furred rib cage.

"You know, she's really too old to do much of anything except get in the way, but the old girl just can't stand being left out of the goings-on around here." Tyler moved his fingers in a circle around the dog's neck. His expression was as tender as his touch. "The other day I carried her along when I went to check on a downed calf Ol' Pete found. Guin can't get herself up into the truck any longer, so I have to lift her into the cab."

"Then you do wait on her hand and foot," Harley said, enchanted by the picture of man and his best friend.

"Oh, yeah. She's got me wrapped around her little paw, don'tcha girl," Tyler said, leaning forward and rubbing his nose against Guin's. He suddenly straightened, avoiding Harley's gaze, and Harley couldn't help but smile.

"Anyway, I lifted her down from the truck and, since she was so tired and all from the ride, she plopped right down for a nap. Only she did her plopping a little too close to the calf for Momma Cow's liking. By the time I heard the ruckus and turned around, Guin had managed to drag herself under the truck, but Momma was still stomping.

"She's got a real bad case of bruised ribs," Tyler explained, sitting back and stretching out his legs. "She's also got enough stitches to give her the look of a patchwork quilt. Her injuries aren't serious. But her spirit's gone."

"You've had her a long time?" Harley asked, watching the dog pull herself halfway into Tyler's lap.

"Gardner gave her to me right after our folks died. She was already about five. Like they say, it's not the years, it's the mileage." Tyler buried his fingers in the ruff of Guin's fur and the dog's eyes drifted shut. "She's put in some long hard ones."

"I never had a pet," Harley said, and when Tyler glanced up added, "You make me wish I had."

"Yeah, well, it's a good thing she can't talk or I'd be in a hell of a lot of trouble. I've told this girl more than I've ever told anyone," Tyler said, his expression darkening. "I really gave Gardner a heck of a rough time the first couple of years after our folks died.

"But I gotta admit that once I got my head outta my butt I realized he was a better dad than our father. He's certainly done a better job managing the place." Ty cleared the pained look from his face and cracked a bold smile. "I figure that's because he knows how to delegate."

"Now why doesn't that surprise me?" Harley teased, thinking of all he'd ordered her to do.

"He's a bossy son of a gun, ain't he?" Tyler laughed. "Jud takes care of the house and the equipment. I take care of the animals and school. The crew manages the stock. And Gardner, well, he takes care of all of us." He glanced up then, sincerity knocking the cocky edge from his expression. "I'm glad to see he finally found someone to take care of him."

"I don't think Gardner needs anyone to take care of him."

"Oh, he needs it all right. He just won't admit it. For some reason he's a real brick wall when it comes to relationships. It's his way or the highway, if you know what I mean."

Oh, yeah. She knew exactly. And was doing her best to make Gardner see what he'd been missing. Harley smiled at the dog's contented wuffle and sigh. "How long until Guin is up and around?"

Tyler eased his legs from beneath the comatose dog. "Physically, she'll heal up in a couple of weeks. She'll never be as good as new. Who would be at ninety? I guess that's what worries me more than anything. Losing someone who's been there for me most of my life." Tyler forced a laugh and looked up at Harley. She saw the little boy in his eyes. "This'll sound stupid, but it's kinda the same way I feel about going to college next fall."

"I'm not sure I understand," Harley prompted.

"You grow used to someone being there, you know. And when you don't have them around every day it throws off your schedule."

Oh, what she would have given to have grown up in a family full of this much love. "Gardner will always be there for you, Ty."

"Yeah, but once I'm off to College Station, who'll be here for him?"

10

"ARE YOU BARNES MEN fattening me up for the kill?" Harley asked, the evening breeze cooling the sun's heat from the air.

"I don't know what you're talking about," Gardner answered, stroking a cherry tomato over Harley's lips—a tomato the same color as her jeans.

Sitting cross-legged on the quilt Gardner had spread beneath the pecan tree, Harley grasped his wrist to still the maddening motion of his hand. She licked the tomato from between his fingers, catching a taste of mesquite smoke and chicken, and Gardner's salty-sweet skin.

She bit down. Juice and seeds spewed into her mouth. "First you feed me monstrously fattening dinners each night. Then breakfasts with enough cholesterol to kill a cow."

His fingers were moving again, roaming, teasing. She tightened her hold. His touch drifted lower. What was it they'd been talking about? "What exactly does Jud do to his biscuits to get them that high?"

"I'm sure your cholesterol doesn't want to know." Lounging on one elbow like some pagan god, Gardner tugged at her lip with the pad of his thumb. "And don't accuse me of being involved in any conspiracy. There's not an ounce of fat in this picnic."

She'd noticed that. That everything he'd packed to eat was low fat, low cholesterol, low calorie. Too bad she had a low appetite.

"You did all right, Barnes. A girl could get used to this kind of attention." Next she'd work on the worship. Then she'd go for the love. She kissed the tip of his thumb. "There's hope for you yet."

"How about hope for us, Harley?" He sat up, shifted closer, threaded his fingers into her hair.

She nearly choked on a tomato seed. "Is it time to get serious?"

For a moment he stared, searching her face, looking deeper than the surface. Then he shook his head. And his eyes said no. "I think it's time for dessert."

The anticipation of splendor. What a beautiful thing. Gardner pulled her mouth close to his. She splayed her hands over his shirt. His breath touched her skin. His muscles quivered beneath her palms.

"I have a need, Harley. It's fierce. Powerful. I've lived with it a long time. But now it's connected to you." He lifted his head and gazed down. His eyes glowed a hot, hot green. "I don't know how to explain it."

"Tell me. Just tell me."

Lips curled up in a racy smile, he dipped his finger in the hollow of her throat. "It started the day I saw a very sexy woman on a plane."

"Sexy? Is that all you saw?"

He sobered then, stilled every motion but the beating of his heart. Her fingers measured the rhythm. The meter matched that of her own.

After a minute he raised his head. "I saw a child, Harley. Our child."

Children. Always children. Her hands slid to her lap. "Gardner, you didn't even know me then. You really don't know me now."

He blinked, banished whatever it was that haunted him. The promise in his eyes raised her spirits—and her temperature.

"I can fix that."

Arousal, like wildfire, raced over her skin. "Sounds like you have a plan."

"What I plan is to do this right, so that every time you take off your clothes you think of me."

Then he took off her clothes.

And while the sun vanished and the moon cast its own pale light from the sky, Gardner worshipped her well and good.

HARLEY LOOKED OUT through the Range Rover's windows at the barest edges of pink-tinted dawn. Gardner lay beside her, his breathing uneven. She wondered if he'd slept at all.

She'd managed to drift and doze, but nothing deeper. It was almost as if her subconscious was counting the hours, determined not to waste a minute in sleep.

They'd climbed into the back of the Rover sometime around midnight after forgoing dessert in favor of each other. They'd talked off and on the hours beyond, sharing secrets and dreams, playing twenty questions and telling knock-knock jokes.

But it was time for the games to stop. She was going home tomorrow and they'd yet to settle a thing.

She rolled onto her side, tucking both hands beneath her chin. "Are you asleep?"

Gardner nodded without opening his eyes.

She leaned over and kissed his thick lashes. The double layer of sleeping bags cushioned her aching bones. But the way she figured, the discomfort of their makeshift bed didn't even rate as a problem. "I want you to do something for me."

Gardner's dimple flashed. "Again?"

Glaring down at his closed eyes, she decided it was a good thing they'd tugged their clothes back on or she might've taken him up on the offer. She couldn't believe how she wanted him.

"No, I want you to close your eyes and tell me what you see."

"My eyes are closed."

"Then keep them that way and tell me what you see."

His dimple deepened. "Hmmm. Red veins on flesh."

Men. Harley rolled her eyes, then cuddled against him and whispered in his ear. "Tell me what you see that keeps you awake."

"I . . . see . . . the future."

Ignoring his crystal-ball sarcasm, Harley parted the plackets of his unsnapped shirt. "How far into the future? Minutes? Days?" She wound a sprig of his chest hair around her finger. "Years, maybe?"

"Hey," he hollered, grabbing for her hand.

"C'mon, Gardner. It's just a little hair," she said and tugged.

"Yeah, but it's got roots. Roots connected to nerves. Nerves connected to muscles. Pull too hard and who knows what might pop up."

In my wildest dreams, she thought, leaning over to taste his skin. "So you're saying that minutes from now things are going to be . . . on the rise?"

He wiggled both brows.

Harley sighed. She could spend a lifetime on Camelot and never get enough of this man. "How about days from now? Start with what will happen Monday, after I'm gone."

A scowl creased his face. "Who said you're leaving?"

"You know I have to."

He captured her fingers and held her hand beneath his. "I don't know anything except that I want you here."

"C'mon, Gardner. Tell me about Monday." She'd never make her point if he kept thwarting her efforts. Or if his heart didn't stop beating so hard in her palm.

"Mondays are always lousy." Gardner snorted. "But without your doom-and-gloom predictions I ought to be able to wallow in my fatty breakfast peacefully."

"Very funny," Harley said, unable to contain a private grin. "What else?"

"I'll more than likely stick to horseback Monday. After last night, the Rover smells too much like you."

Harley breathed deep. "I think it smells like us."

Gardner's hand tightened around her fingers. He was silent for several moments, then shook his head. "All those hours in the saddle are going to be tough without someone to work out the kinks when I get home."

Harley didn't even want to think about anyone else working out Gardner's kinks. "What about supper?"

"Oh, I'll get to hear a blow-by-blow of everything that went wrong with Jud and Ty's day. Then they'll grill me like a steak, asking why I couldn't talk you into staying." He grunted. "Monday's going to be a bitch."

"Poor baby." Harley snuggled deeper into his side, pulling her edge of the sleeping bag over her back. She rubbed her socks against Gardner's. "Let's see if you can predict five years into the future."

"Hell, that's easy. I see you and me and—" he squinted his closed eyes "—what was the time frame? Five years?"

"Yes," she whispered, pulling in a shaky breath.

"You, me and three children camped under this tree. The kids are sleeping. Two of them have blond hair. One's darker, but his eyes are as blue as yours." Gardner laid a hand low on her belly. "And the one you're carrying will look just like me."

Harley's heart slammed against her chest. She had trouble finding her voice. "We'll be living here, then?"

He nodded, tucked both hands beneath his head. "The house will be full of your antiques. I'll have to enlarge the stock pens and maybe add on to the barn. The kids have to have horses, you know."

No. She didn't know.

"We'll have high chairs and cribs and tiny hats and boots scattered everywhere. The kids'll have surrogate uncles coming out their ears. I can see it all, Harley. The perfect family."

"Like the family you have now?"

He hesitated a minute. "What's wrong with the family I have now?"

"Not a thing. I just want to know what you think keeps you, Tyler and Jud together."

"Blood. The commitment that comes from that. Respect. Honor." He shrugged. "Those things are all a part of being a family."

"What about love?"

He came fully awake then. So fast, in fact, that when he levered up on his elbow, Harley fell back and hit her head. He hovered over her, his eyes stark and frightening. "I've seen love in my lifetime, Harley. You want to hear about it?

"You want to hear about a father who stares his son blankly in the eye as if he can't remember his name? You want to hear about a husband who gets soused night after night and sleeps off his drunk on his wife's grave?

"You want to hear about a man who loves his wife so much that when she dies he decides to go with her and leave his two sons behind?"

Harley felt the first stinging tears trail over her temples and into her hair. She reached up to press her fingers to his lips, but her hands trembled, and he dodged her touch, anyway. "That's not love, Gardner."

"Damn right it's not. There's no such thing."

"But there is," she insisted.

"No. I don't believe there's a single healthy emotion that gives one person such destructive control over another."

His gaze softened and he worried a wayward strand of her hair. "I do believe in you and me. I believe we have a future. I can give you security, happiness, financial stability. And I can give you children.

"But I cannot give you what I don't have to give."

GARDNER WASN'T SURE if what he felt was sorrow, but nothing about this parting was sweet. With one hand gripping the frame of the Blazer's window, the other splayed flat on the roof, he stood in the open doorway between Harley and goodbye.

He needed to step back and let her go. Just let her go. Easier said than done.

"You know, Gardner," she began, her mouth twisted into a wry smile. "I'm not going to make it very far with **you hanging** on to the door that way."

He wasn't ready for her to leave. He didn't think he'd convinced her of anything but that he wanted her in his bed. Rolling the tightness from his shoulders, he said, "I don't know. Might give the highway patrol something to talk about."

"I can see the headlines." Harley diagramed a banner in the air. "Rancher Ropes Runaway Steer—ing Wheel."

Gardner groaned. "Very funny."

Her expression changed, growing sober. She toyed with the buttons on his khaki shirt. "You knew this week wouldn't last forever, Gardner."

Had he? He glanced over the top of the Blazer to collect his thoughts. "What time do you think you'll get home?"

Slipping the tips of her fingers between the gaps of his shirt, she shrugged. "With good weather and good roads, I'll be there by eight."

"I'll call you at ten," he managed, her nails rasping over the hair on his belly.

"You don't have to do that."

"Yes." He looked back down, watched her fingers move underneath his shirt. "I do."

"Checking up on your latest investment?" she asked, one eyebrow arched.

It would be so simple if that's all she was. "You know it's more than that."

"Do I?" Her question was only a breath.

It was more. How much, he was afraid to say. "I'll feel better knowing you got home safely."

"Then let me give you a quick call when I get there."

"No. I'll call you at ten. That'll give you time to get unpacked and wind down."

"What if I'm asleep?"

Head cocked to one side, Gardner leaned in close and captured her hand. "You ought to know by now that I'm worth waking up for."

"You and Tyler." She laughed, tugging her fingers free. "I sure will miss my daily dose of Barnes ego."

"No. You won't." Reaching up, Gardner fingered a flyaway lock of her hair.

"What? Are you sending Tyler to live with me?"

He narrowed both eyes. "Let's keep Tyler out of this discussion."

"C'mon, Gardner." She laid her hand against his cheek. "I'm just trying to keep things light."

The problem in a nutshell. He wasn't feeling light at all. In fact, he was feeling pretty damned depressed. He'd felt this down only once before—the day his father had chosen pills over his boys, leaving Gardner no chance to ask why. "Damn."

"What is it?"

What it was was a realization he didn't want to consider. "It's nothing. Look. I better get on back. I've got a lot of work to catch up on."

Her expression fell. Her lashes drifted down. And then she looked up and over his shoulder.

How many things besides hurting her feelings did he regret? "I didn't mean—"

"No, you're right. I've neglected a lot this week, too."

"Was it worth it?" he asked, hating to.

She answered with a nod. "I didn't realize I'd been working so hard, or that I needed a break."

"A break?"

"How about a purely pleasurable distraction?"

He thumbed up the brim of his hat. "Now I'm a distraction?"

With one wrist draped over the steering wheel, she offered him an impudent grin. "The best I've ever had."

"When can you arrange to be distracted again?"

"Not for a while, I'm afraid. The holiday season is coming up. It's my busiest time." She shrugged, her smile apologetic. "You know, that lay-of-the-land thing. Golden's Touch comes first."

Why did his own words—hell, his own excuse— sound so lame coming from Harley? He understood, but his spirits refused to be lifted. "How does the future look from where you're sitting?"

"I don't know." Her sigh was long and slow. "That's something we're both going to have to think about."

"Why don't you think about this, instead..." Threading his fingers into her hair, he cupped her head and sought her mouth. He knew her taste, the flavor of her need, the heady press of her body seeking his.

His heart slammed his chest with a painful blow, and he knew the greatest urge to scoop Harley from her seat and take her down to the ground.

His desire was primal, raw, the basic hunger of a man for his mate. Survival and creation. The earth, the wind, the rain. Everything he felt, he'd fought against for a lifetime.

Harley Golden lived beneath his skin. And now he knew his father's pain.

"DELIVERY TIME."

Holding the brown-paper package under one arm, Mona waggled her way down the center aisle from the front of the store to the back. Bleary-eyed, Harley watched her assistant's hip-swaying progress. Mona's thematic dress of the day had gone too far.

With every tiny step she took, Mona clanged and rattled like Marley's ghost. Though bondage and antiques made for a strangely eclectic mix, Harley had to admit that Mona pulled off the combination with a Madonnaesque flair. Trimmed with ancient coins and links of chain, her bullet-studded bustier and black patent mini sucked up to her curves like white on rice.

Rice. Harley shuddered at the thought. For three days she'd been suffering the stomach virus from hell, and rice was the only food she'd managed to keep down.

Life held no justice. Here she'd finished Dr. Fisher's account and couldn't even wallow in her success. Only in misery.

"Who's this one from?" she mumbled, cheek flat against the cool wooden surface of her desk. Mona read the name from the label, and Harley poofed out a sigh.

"One would think you might show more enthusiasm at receiving the final piece to Dr. F.'s contract," Mona admonished.

"You want to see enthusiasm? I'll show you enthusiasm." One finger crooked in a come-hither curl, Harley squinted up at Mona.

The box balanced in the V of her elbows, Mona formed a crucifix using both index fingers. "You can keep your little germies all to yourself, thank you very much. I have a wedding to plan and I don't intend to let anything stand in the way."

Harley had returned from Camelot a month ago to find that Gibson had indeed popped the question. And since Gibson didn't do jewelry, Mona had decided to forgo the traditional engagement ring and wedding set. She'd had her nose pierced with a diamond stud instead.

"I don't know. I think your complexion could use more color. I'll be glad to share my yellow."

"No thank you. The wedding will be black-and-white. Not bumblebee."

"Did I mention how happy I am for you?" Harley managed a thin-in-momentum-but-abundant-in-sincerity smile. Every woman deserved the chance at such incredible joy.

"I'm happy for me, too." A look of supreme contentment softened Mona's features.

Harley closed her eyes, ready to wallow in what-might-have-beens and Gardner—until Mona moved. She clanked and clattered her way to Harley's desk.

"Now, I'll just set this box behind your desk. When Dr. F. stops by, I'll point him in your direction."

"Give it here." Harley managed to lift her head. And to keep it on her shoulders. "You know Dr. Fischer. If I don't bestow my seal of approval in advance, he'll find the tiniest scratch and call it damage instead of age."

Mona handed over the package and hovered nearby while Harley rummaged in a desk drawer for a box cutter. "Getting a little too close to my germies, wouldn't you say?"

Propping her hip on the edge of Harley's desk, Mona shook her head. "I was kidding about the germs. I'm naturally immune."

"All your shots up-to-date, huh?"

"Very funny." Mona scowled.

Harley groaned, the box cutter slipping from her hands.

"Whatever's wrong with you is affecting your motor control." Mona reached out. "Quit moaning and give me the box."

"I need a vacation." Harley sank into her chair.

With a couple of swift strokes, Mona finished Harley's botched job. "You just had a vacation."

Harley shook her head, then regretted doing so when Mona's pointed breasts became four, then six. "No. I need a real vacation. Sand, sun and no Dr. Fischer."

"What? No wild-West show? No dude ranch? No dudes?" Mona added the last with a wiggle of both brows. The diamond in her nose reflected the overhead light.

Harley had never thought of the Barnes men as dudes. *Dude* gave her the impression of big-city boys portraying cowboy-for-a-day. Tyler and Jud may have joked while they worked, but she'd never seen them play. And the only playing Gardner had done involved feathers and cherry tomatoes and . . .

"You're flushed, Harley. Do you have a fever?"

"I'm fine," she answered, feeling feverish and missing Gardner like she couldn't believe. These past four weeks of phone calls had lasted forever.

The day she'd left Camelot she should've told Gardner she'd arrange to be distracted anytime, anywhere. That all he had to do was call.

Oh, he'd called, all right. He'd talked his sexy talk, turned her ache into an obsession and more than managed each and every time to distract her from the issue at hand.

Love.

Mona laid the back of her hand over Harley's forehead. "You don't feel hot."

"I told you I'm fine." To prove it, Harley got to her feet. Slowly, but she managed. "Here, hold the box still while I trash the packing."

"What is it?" Mona asked.

Harley peeled away the layer of bubble wrap. "A doctor's bag, circa 1920."

"Dr. F. will love this," Mona remarked as Harley turned the bag from side to side.

Not as much as he would have loved the one in Gardner's attic, Harley thought.

The one Gardner kept as a manacle, shackling him to his past. He'd never spoken of the future, their future, except in regard to continuing the Barnes family name.

How romantic, Harley silently mused. *Come live with me and be my... brood mare.*

"Harley, you really don't look so good."

Harley pushed off her depressing thoughts. "I'm just tired. Between Dr. Fischer and Mrs. Mitchmore, this last month has been a killer."

"Then go upstairs and rest. The bag looks perfect. And I can handle Dr. Fischer."

Mona's offer was heaven to Harley's ears. As was the thought of bed and quilt and pillows and sheets. She wanted nothing more than to curl into a tiny ball and sleep the rest of the day away.

She glanced down at her watch. It was only four o'clock. Still ... "Are you sure you don't mind?"

"Would I offer if I did?"

"No." Harley patted Mona's fishnet-clad knee. "You're one of the only truly honest people I know."

Leaning forward, Mona nodded, her eyes narrowing to slits of intensity. Or was it eyeliner? "That's because I've learned to be totally honest with myself first."

Hmmm. Another trait certain people could stand to learn. "Then if we're being honest here, Mona, can we talk about your clothes?"

Standing, Mona pressed her palms on the outside curve of both breasts. "How Madonna pulls this off I'll never know. I feel like the prow of a Viking ship."

At that, Harley left, leaving Mona instructions on how to handle Dr. Fischer. Feeling only moderately guilty, she trudged up her stairs, dragging her weary body behind her. A hundred thousand pounds couldn't weigh any more than her feet.

She'd just stripped down to her panties, pulled on a wash-worn University of Texas T-shirt and curled up beneath three inches of antique quilt into that oh-so-comforting, self-hugging ball when her phone rang.

She knew it was Gardner. Without moving a muscle, without taking a breath, without another thought, she knew it was Gardner.

His pursuit had become intense in nature, weakening her driving need to have him declare his love. A weakness she was finding hard to counter with her convenient list of rationalizations. A weakness she resented. She was so damned close to giving in.

Before the answering machine picked up, she did.

"'Lo?" she mumbled.

"You don't sound a lot better than you did last night."

Ignoring the roller-coaster rumble through her stomach, Harley pressed her fingers to the base of her throat. "This too shall pass."

"Well, if it doesn't I want you to go to the doctor."

Since she felt like warm death, anyway, his comment just settled in wrong. "I've been nursing myself through colds and worse for thirty years. I think I'm the best judge of whether or not I need a doctor."

"Only if you're thinking clearly."

Harley bristled. "Are you saying I'm not?"

Gardner took a very long minute to reply. Not a good sign so early in this conversation.

"You know, Harley," he finally responded, "I didn't call to argue."

"I know. I'm sorry." And she truly was. Eyes closed, she slowly counted to ten. "You caught me half-asleep. I wasn't expecting to hear from you tonight since we talked yesterday."

"No, Harley. I talked. You mumbled and moaned, which is one of the reasons I called back. To see if you're feeling any better. Obviously, you're not."

"These things usually last two or three days. I'm sure I'll be fine tomorrow."

"If not, will you consider seeing the doctor?"

"I'll consider it."

"But you won't promise."

"C'mon, Gardner." Harley rolled onto her back and drew her knees to her chest, focusing on the repetitive circle the ceiling fan sketched overhead. "It's just a bug. Nothing serious."

"As long as you're sure." Gardner verbally conceded the battle, though his tone wasn't acquiescent at all.

Harley didn't know whether to feel annoyed or triumphant. Who she was speaking to? Camelot's boss or her lover? "Hmmm. All this concern. A girl might get the feeling that you cared."

"I do care, Harley."

She knew that. Just like she knew she was feeling like crud and taking it out on him. "Let's chalk this up to a rotten day and start over. Did you call for a reason other than to hear my lovely voice?"

"Well, if that's the reason I called, I'd sure as hell be disappointed, wouldn't I?" Irritation seeped into his tone.

Harley rubbed her temples with forefinger and thumb. First her stomach. Now her head. She couldn't handle a blow to her heart. "Gardner, why are we doing this?"

"I'd lay odds that frustration is at the top of the list. The phone calls just don't cut it anymore. And before you snap my head off again I'm talking about more than sex. I miss you, Harley."

Harley tucked the quilt to her chin, the phone to her ear and curled into herself for comfort. She wanted him—no, the way she felt right now, she *needed* him to say more. She needed him to say that he wished he were here to take care of her, to hold her close until the ache went away.

But the missing her was a good start. And a good sign. She released a heart-deep sigh. "I miss you, too."

"It was the strangest feeling watching you drive away," he went on, as if he hadn't heard. "I kept thinking that you shouldn't be leaving, that you belong here, that you had as much reason, as much *right*, to be on Camelot as Jud or Tyler or me.

"It was hard work convincing myself that we hadn't known each other long enough for me to be feeling that way."

"And did you?" she asked, the bud of hope blooming.

"What?"

"Convince yourself?" she asked again, the bloom unfurling.

"No."

Harley released a pent-up breath, only to find it difficult to draw another. How could a single, two-letter word say so much?

Gardner inhaled slowly and Harley tensed, waiting and waiting and waiting to hear.

"I think I've known you forever," he finally managed, his voice low, controlled, yet passionate in intent. "It seems like you've been a part of my life since before we met. How do you explain something like that, Harley?"

By calling it love, she wanted to scream, but didn't. Not when he'd voiced a vulnerability he'd no doubt deny.

"If you were here now, I could take care of you," Gardner said, then offered a short, shaky laugh. "We could skip the bacon and eggs and go straight for a healthy dose of oatmeal."

"And a couple of Jud's biscuits?" Harley added, determined to make the most of this connection before he resurrected his wall of male stubbornness.

"Biscuits, pancakes, French toast, muffins, you name it. Whatever you need to get you back on your feet."

"Does that include some TLC?" she asked wistfully.

"As much as you can handle, honey," he said, his tone shot through with supreme satisfaction. "Breakfast, lunch and dinner in bed. Back rubs. Long, hot bubble baths. And a hug and kiss for good measure."

"You make a tempting offer, Gardner Barnes."

"Which is exactly my intent, Harley Golden. I don't like to think about you being alone when you're sick."

"And the rest of the time?"

"The rest of the time I prefer you that way. Unless I'm the one keeping you company."

"That's some kind of possessive streak you've got there," Harley teased, feeling a bit smothered, but thinking that she liked it.

"Damn right I'm possessive. Of everything that's mine. I take care of my own."

Which meant he'd take care of her, of that she had no doubt. But how close did that come to love? Didn't his offer encompass everything love was? Everything but the words? Could she live with that?

Pushing aside her fevered musings, Harley responded to Gardner's claim. "If all that bathtub-and-back-rub talk is your way of taking care, then I'd say this discussion deserves further consideration."

"How does next week sound?"

"Too far away. Why not tomorrow night when I'm feeling better?"

"Because next week we can do it in person." When Harley caught a breath, Gardner laughed. "I'll be in Houston for a meeting Friday. I want to spend the rest of the weekend with you."

"Another date?"

"No. This one's a definite seduction," he growled. "I want to see where you work. I want to see where you live. But don't plan on showing me the city. The only tour I want is the shortest route from your place back to my hotel."

"No. I want you to stay here. With me. I want you to see what you're getting yourself into." *I want you to see why my life-style is not compatible with raising a family. I want you to make your decision then, not judge me on what's gone on before.*

"What I'm getting myself into, huh? Does that mean you're thinking long-range?"

"Let's just say the possibilities at this point are endless." *And I have not yet begun to fight.*

ONCE HE'D CRADLED the receiver, Gardner reached for the report he'd tossed on his bedside table. Having Harley investigated had been a gut reaction, a business decision, but one made weeks ago.

Before he knew her. Before she'd become more than business to him, more than the means to an end.

He scanned the typed lines for a second time, then spun the single-spaced sheet toward the bed. The investigation had turned up nothing; reading the summary proved a waste of time. Time better spent adjusting the sprung hinge on Merlin's stall, he thought, shrugging back into his sweat-damp shirt.

He should have saved himself the effort of opening the envelope in the first place. Nothing the investigator revealed came as any surprise. But why would it? She'd been open and honest with him from the first, trusting in spite of her irresponsible parents.

So what's your excuse, pal?

Gardner rubbed the ache behind his eyes. He'd never thought himself the type to get caught up in an obsession. But what else could he call the tightening in his chest, the fierce burning pain in his gut, each time Harley came to mind?

If he called it love, he'd be as weak as his father. And though Tyler or Jud or Camelot may have borne the brunt of his faults, making the mistake that destroyed his father had never been a concern.

One thing in his life had been a given. He'd made damn sure to become a stronger man than one who threw away life on an intangible emotion called love.

LATER THAT EVENING Gardner walked into the den, the investigator's report rolled tight in one hand. He braced his forearm on the mantel, tapped the tube of paper against the polished wood and watched the low-burning flames lick away at the first dry wood of fall.

Resin popped and ashes settled. Sweet smoke plumed. Tiny sparks drifted, lighting the firebox like fireflies blinking bright in the prairie night.

"Thought a little fire might take the nip out of the room."

Gardner glanced around. Behind him, Jud shifted in his recliner, adjusting the woolen throw spread over his lap.

"Are you feeling any better?" Gardner asked.

Placing a strip of leather between the pages of his Louis L'Amour Western, Jud removed his bifocals, folded them, then set both book and glasses on the table at his side.

"Nothing that a shot of Maalox wouldn't cure. Or better yet, Jack Daniel's." Pressing his fist to his stomach, he smiled up at Gardner. "Sometimes I can't remember why I gave up drinking."

"I remember," Gardner answered, taking in the exhaustion etched around his uncle's eyes. "And I guarantee you need rest more than whiskey. Sounds like you've got a touch of the same thing Harley does."

"Ahhh," Jud began, drawing the word out meaningfully. "So you two are still talking."

Shoulders back, Gardner forced away the familiar tension creeping into his bones. "Any reason we shouldn't be?"

Jud shook his head. "Not a one comes to mind. But you haven't made mention of the girl since she went home. That's all."

"Last I looked, I was entitled to a private life."

"Which is why I haven't asked."

Frustration riding high and hard, Gardner dropped down to sit on the edge of the hearth. He was being a jerk, and Jud deserved better. Besides, he preferred to use his uncle as a sounding board—not a punching bag.

Elbows braced on his knees, Gardner twisted the report between both fists and exhaled. Even putting the thought into words was tough. "Harley doesn't want kids, Jud."

"No crime in that." Jud lifted one brow, deflecting the defensive comeback hovering on Gardner's tongue. "Has she told you why?"

"She said the demands of her career limit the time she'd have to put in raising a family."

Lowering the recliner's footrest, Jud sat forward. "Sounds like the girl's got a good head on her shoulders."

"Which is why she'd make such a great mother," Gardner replied, twisting the paper tighter. "She even talked about turning her antique business into a hobby."

"You mean if she had a husband to do the providing?"

"Yeah."

Jud sloughed off the blanket, gave it a quick fold and stuffed it under the lamp table before turning his keen gaze Gardner's way. "Then her career isn't all that's standing in the way?"

Gardner's gaze dropped to the floor. "No."

"So what's the problem?"

"She wants more than stability or financial security." Which was the hardest part to accept. That an intangible stood in the way of his goal. "In her words, she wants everything."

"You mean she wants love." Jud propped his forearms on his knees. "I was hoping you and Tyler would be the ones to break this curse."

Frowning, Gardner asked, "What curse?"

"The Barnes men just never have gotten it right. We either love too much, like your dad, or not at all."

"Like you," Gardner stated, curiosity building.

"It's a weakness, either way you look at it."

Gardner let out a snort. "You're about the last man I'd ever call weak."

"Guess that depends on your definition. I sure wasn't strong enough to stand up for what I wanted."

"A woman?"

A wry grin brought a dimple to Jud's whiskered cheek. "What else?"

Rising, Gardner paced the short length of the hearth. "You've never said anything. In all these years. I had no idea you'd been involved with anyone special."

"Like you said, we're all entitled to a private life."

Touché. "And you gave up yours to look after Ty and me."

"Taking on you and Ty isn't the reason I ended up alone. In fact, bringing up you boys helped keep me from going off the deep end any worse than I did with the drinking. That's what family's all about."

"I'm glad *you* managed to see it that way."

"Gardner," Jud began, reaching out one hand to slow Gardner's troubled stride. "Don't let your father's weakness become yours."

"That's one thing you don't need to worry about. I have no intention of falling in love."

"That's exactly what I mean."

Gardner finally stopped, his back to the fire. "I don't understand."

"Love didn't destroy your father. He destroyed himself. When your mother died, he quit. Just gave up on everything." Jud's gaze took on a faraway look, focused not on Gardner but on years gone by.

"He'd been a stubborn man before he married. A mulish, hell-raising kid before that. And you can't tell me that down inside he couldn't have found that old cussedness and used it to make it through."

"Then he *was* weak." Gardner bit off the accusation, crushing the tube of paper he still held in one fist.

"Only because he didn't try."

"And what about you?"

Piercing and shrewd despite his illness, Jud's gaze honed in on Gardner's. "I took the easy way out. Same as you."

"I don't know if I want to hear this," Gardner mumbled, turning to the side and slanting a glance at the fire.

"I'm sure you don't. But you need to before you make the same mistakes I did."

Jud joined Gardner at the hearth. With one fist braced on the mantel, he stirred up the ashes. The tip of the poker glowed as red as the coals by the time he set it back in the stand.

"I saw what your mother did to your dad. I don't know if it came from insecurity or pure devotion, but the woman wouldn't make a move without him.

"She carried him lunch every day, stayed with him while he ate, then, more often than not, the two of them disappeared for the rest of the afternoon. Even on her weekly trips to town for supplies she wanted him along."

"And he went."

"That he did. Turning his back on business, and you boys, to be at her beck and call."

"And she had it just as bad." Gardner propped one boot on the hearth, feeling Jud's gaze with the same intensity as the heat from the blaze. "She didn't have time for anyone else. Especially not for Tyler or me."

"Considering all you've gone through, it's not surprising you hold some resentment."

"Resentment?" Gardner heaved a disgusted snort, the leaping flames failing to soothe, only reminding him again of the heat Harley stirred in his soul. "That's a word that barely begins to cover what I feel."

"Or what you don't feel."

He cast a sideways glance at his uncle. "What's that cryptic remark supposed to mean?"

"That you're all business, Gardner. You think with your head, and never with your heart."

"A fact I'm damned proud of."

"So was I, once upon a time. After seeing what your folks did to each other, not to mention to you and Ty, and thinking I know everything, which most of the time I do," Jud added with a weak grin, "I decided years before your father's funeral that no woman would ever trap me."

"Sounds like a smart decision."

"So I thought at the time."

Gardner took in the look of regret aging Jud's expression. "Then one did."

"Yeah. One did." Rubbing a hand down his jaw, Jud returned to his chair. Once seated, he stared up at Gardner. "And I gnawed off my own leg to get away."

Gardner absorbed Jud's words; their meaning hit too close to home. "You regret it?"

"I'm still limping, boy."

"You think about her a lot?" Gardner asked, wondering when a day would pass that he didn't think of Harley.

"Every day of my life," Jud answered, reaching for the woolen throw and tucking it around his thighs.

That's what he'd thought. No, what he'd feared. He tossed the report on the fire, and watched the flames reduce the paper to fine ash. "What was her name?"

"Ellie." Jud settled back in the chair. His lashes drifted down. "And she had the prettiest bluebonnet eyes."

GARDNER STEPPED INSIDE Golden's Touch with Harley on his mind. Turning to close the door, he caught sight of the front window's seasonal display and smiled.

Miniature wooden elves and antique ornaments hung on lace ribbons from a garland of pine boughs with the same sense of whimsy he'd heard in Harley's voice when she'd talked about loving Christmas.

He was going to have to think of something to get her. A gift as original as the bed her parents sent. Or as sensually extravagant as the presents she received from her sister.

One glance around the store told him she didn't need anything in the way of antiques. That would make as much sense as giving Jud a leather-bound set of Louis L'Amour novels. No matter the value, a gift wasn't a gift if you couldn't enjoy it. Or if it didn't come with a piece of the giver attached. Damn, but he was philosophical these days.

Hearing the click of heels on the buffed wooden floor, Gardner tensed, but it wasn't Harley he smelled. He schooled his features into a pleasant expression, and glanced around into the face of an exquisitely beautiful woman.

"May I help you, sir?" she asked, her ink black hair swinging to frame her jaw.

Nice legs, he thought to himself, taking in the short length of her suit skirt. The ivory lace did exotic things to her figure and face. But she wasn't Harley.

And he wanted Harley. "I'm looking for Miss Golden."

The woman's smile was genuine, but cautious. "I'm sorry, Miss Golden is unavailable at the moment. May I leave her a message?"

Unavailable? Not likely. "We have an appointment."

Frowning, the woman turned away. "She didn't mention an appointment to me. Let me check her calendar."

Gardner followed her to the rolltop desk set up in a corner of the store. She flipped through the wire-bound pages of Harley's calendar, and ran one nail over each line of today's date.

"I'm sorry. Miss Golden didn't make a notation of your appointment. In fact, it appears she has the next three days clear."

Exactly. "I'm that appointment."

"Ah." Mischievousness lit her almond-shaped eyes, though her demeanor remained all business. "Then you must be Mr. Barnes. I'm Mona Tedrick, Harley's assistant."

Gardner shook her offered hand, detecting a challenge in the firm grip—and doing his best to overlook the diamond stud in her nose. "Where can I find Harley?"

Pursing her lips, Mona pulled free. "Then she didn't tell you?"

"Tell me what?"

Mona's gaze was steady and direct. Almost too direct. "I'm sure she meant to call you last night, but her change in plans came up so suddenly. I'm not surprised that she forgot a few details."

Gardner wasn't a detail. "Miss Tedrick, is it? I'm afraid I'm going to have to insist on knowing more. Where is Harley?"

Her shift to nervousness was so subtle Gardner would have missed it had he not been looking her square in the face. "I'm afraid I can't say."

"I assure you Harley doesn't need protection from me."

"I guess that's a matter of opinion," Mona mumbled, before once again assuming her efficient air. She laced her fingers at her waist. "There is an illness in the family. Miss Golden will not be back at work full-time for at least another month."

This had gone on long enough. "I don't care when she'll be back to work. Our relationship has nothing to do with business. I want to know where she is now."

"I'm afraid I'm not at liberty to tell you."

"Then I'll have to find out for myself." Gardner rounded the corner of the desk.

Mona stepped into his path. "I'm sorry, sir. Her apartment is off-limits."

"Not to me."

"The door is locked."

"Was locked," Gardner countered, finding his way blocked by an armoire and an angry woman.

Mona's hackles rose higher. "Mr. Barnes."

"Miss Tedrick." Gardner forced a calm he didn't feel.

"Look, buster," Mona began, tossing her head. "I don't know who you think you're dealing with here, but you take another step and it'll be the last painless one you ever take," she vowed, shaking a wicked-looking wine-tipped fingernail in his face.

And that's when he saw the tattoo on her inner wrist. A quarter moon and a tiny star sat on the tongue of a dragon—a dragon whose body disappeared under an elegant ivory sleeve.

Great. Just great. He was dealing with a maniac.

"Mona?"

Mona whirled at the sound of Harley's voice. Gardner grinned triumphantly.

"Did you go by the pharmacy?"

Harley's voice sounded weak. Gardner panicked. Mona spun around. "Stay right here, bucko."

"Don't even think you can stop me, dragon lady."

He reached the staircase one step behind Mona, only to find Harley slumped in a sitting position halfway between the bottom and the top. Her hair hung lifeless around her sunken cheeks; the circles above her cheekbones shone bluer than her eyes.

He afforded Mona the briefest glance. "This is the illness in the family?"

She had the grace to blush before she nodded.

"You have medicine she needs?"

Mona's hand fluttered. "It's on the desk."

"Get it. Now." He stomped up the stairs, scooped Harley into his arms, then finished the climb. "Which way to the bedroom?"

When Harley pointed, he headed in that direction, picking up no details of her home, only the impression of light and air. Lowering her to sit on the edge of the rumpled bed, Gardner knelt before her. "You've been sick all this time and you haven't told me?"

Weakly she grinned, and laid her icy palm along his cheek. "Hi, Gardner. I've missed you, too."

"Lord, Harley. Why didn't you tell me?"

"I didn't want to bother you."

He brushed back her hair, feeling his heart catch. He couldn't even find the strength to offer a reassuring smile. "You never bother me."

"I took your advice. I went to the doctor." She licked her dry lips, and Gardner reached for the water glass on her bedside table. "What I'm feeling will pass in another couple of months."

"Months?" Oh, God. "What is it?"

"Morning sickness." She smiled, crossing her arms over her stomach. "I just happen to be one of the ones who suffers all day long."

"You're pregnant?" he barely managed to whisper.

"I'm pregnant."

Oh, God. He couldn't breathe. He couldn't see.

He knuckled a thumb in the corner of one eye. "How bad is the morning sickness?"

She showed him. All over his new ostrich-skin boots. He couldn't even mind.

SITTING AT HER dining table in one of four ice-cream parlor chairs, Harley hugged her knees to her chest. The hem of her fuzzy nightgown trailed over the sherbet yellow seat cushion. The toes of her fuzzy slippers peeked from under the edge of her raspberry pink chenille robe. And her stomach sizzled with a fuzzy feeling that had nothing to do with pregnancy and everything to do with Gardner being in her soda-fountain kitchen.

She hadn't wanted him to find out this way. She'd planned to tell him, of course. Eventually. Once she got used to the concept of motherhood. And the idea—no, the *reality* of having a baby. Once she figured out the best time, the best place, the best words.

Upchucking on his boots had saved her the hassle.

He hadn't let her out of his sight for a minute since, even sending Mona to his rental car for his bags. A little disconcerting, Harley had decided, being checked on while she bathed. But as Gardner had told her, it was a little late in the game for modesty. And way past time for truth.

When he set a bowl of Cream of Wheat on the table, Harley tentatively inhaled. After a week of nothing but noxious odors, she was afraid to breathe without a painter's mask over her nose. The gruel, believe it or not, smelled wonderful.

Pulling the bowl closer, she thought she might actually have a few vomit-free hours ahead. A good thing since she wanted to enjoy Gardner's visit. And especially since they had so much to discuss.

He'd hardly uttered a meaningful word since she'd christened his new boots, and she wondered what he was thinking . . . if he'd changed his mind about wanting children, if he'd changed his mind about wanting her.

The sleeves of his dress shirt cuffed up, Gardner draped a dish towel over the back of a second chair. He gripped the curved railing with both hands and nodded toward the bowl. "I wasn't sure what to add. Or what you could stomach."

She didn't want to risk the combined aroma of maple syrup and butter any more than she wanted to risk making a wrong move until she and Gardner had talked. "Brown sugar will be fine."

Rummaging through her pantry, Gardner picked up the box of sugar, then a canister of tea bags. He shook the small oval tin. "How 'bout some hot tea?"

"Sounds great."

He handed her the box, then set about brewing tea. Harley sprinkled a drifting of sugar over the cereal and watched Gardner move. Jealously, she admired the way his jeans made themselves at home on his lower body. And she remembered too well the way his thighs and backside had drawn taut in her palms.

He reached into the cupboard for a mug. His crisp oxford-cloth shirt reached with him, defining tendons and muscles and a lean, natural strength. When he moved, his walk was loose; when he paused, his stance was suggestive. And always, always, his masculine sensuality was effortless. His body was a blueprint for every woman's fantasy, and Harley's stomach tumbled.

When he placed the steaming mug on the table, she still hadn't touched her cereal. Her hands were shaking too badly to do so. Blaming her nerves on her sickness, she fluttered her fingers in an encompassing gesture. "Is this some of the TLC you were talking about?"

Gardner spun and straddled the chair beside her, then reached for her spoon. Stirring the melted sugar into the cereal, he said, "Not bad for a guy who's never been in your kitchen before."

Harley propped her elbow on the table, her chin on her palm, though all she really wanted to do was touch his hair, his face, the curl of his ear. "At least you're not the kind of guy who doesn't think he belongs in a kitchen at all."

"That's Jud's doing. He's a stickler for dividing up chores." Scooping up a spoonful of cereal, he scraped the back over the edge of the bowl. "You feel like eatin' now?"

She nodded and he lifted the spoon. Meeting his gaze, she opened her mouth, remembering the way he tasted, the way he kissed.

"What was the stuff the doctor sent you?"

Licking her lips, Harley swallowed. "An over-the-counter medicine to settle the nausea. But even though he's assured me it's safe, I don't want to take it too often."

"You've suffered like this for a month without taking anything?"

"The first three weeks weren't bad at all. But this last one's been rough. I tried the soda crackers routine and every other home remedy imaginable. The doctor told me to try this medicine. I don't know which is worse. The taste of the medicine or throwing up." Harley squeezed her knees tighter and grimaced. "And just think. Only ten or so weeks to go."

"How are you going to manage between now and then?"

"I'm pregnant, Gardner, not disabled. And I've got Mona to take up the slack."

His brows a slash of concentration, Gardner tapped the spoon on the lip of the bowl. "I'm not crazy about you working when you're this sick."

Harley rested her fingertips on the back of his hand; tiny tufts of hair tickled her skin. Please, God, let me do this right. "I'm going to take care of the baby, Gardner. Don't worry."

He tap-tap-tapped the spoon on the bowl, finally shoving it into the cereal before raking an angry hand over his hair. "If I hadn't shown up here today, Harley, the way I did, would you have told me about the baby?"

"Oh, Gardner, of course I would have." She squeezed his wrist; his pulse quickened. "How can you even ask such a thing?"

"You said you didn't want kids." His tone flat, emotionless, he looked her straight in the eye.

In a disembodied motion, Harley slowly withdrew her hand, searching for her voice—and an ounce of understanding. "You thought I'd get rid of this one? Behind your back? Don't you know me better than that?"

He had the decency to look ashamed.

"That's what I thought," she said, not feeling the least bit smug. Only hugely disappointed. "Yes, I planned to tell you. But discussing this subject requires more energy than I've had lately."

"So you decided you would wait to tell me. Even if it took another, what was the figure—" he inquired sarcastically "—ten weeks?"

She refused to jump to the bait. "Yes, Gardner. Even if it took that long. This baby's not going anywhere. And neither are you or I."

Gardner shoved the bowl away, nearly toppling the cereal in the center of the table. "What now?"

Harley tugged her robe down over her toes. This conversation was not going any of the ways she'd imagined it might. "My immediate plans don't include anything more involved than making it through one day at a time."

One brow lifted tyrannically, Gardner cast her a sideways glance. "You're not planning any more buying trips."

"No, not for a while."

"That wasn't a question." One corner of his mouth quirked up a bit.

Harley marginally relaxed. "Well, then, since you *didn't* ask, I'll tell you, anyway. Mona is more than capable of handling the store. I know what our Christmas buyers want and have already stocked up. Now it's just a matter of sitting back and letting the merchandise sell itself."

"And you can do that from up here, in your bed?"

"Only on the days I absolutely can't sit at my desk," she offered with a soothing smile. "But once this twenty-four-hour-a-day morning sickness passes, I plan to work as long as I can."

"What about after that, Harley? What happens after the baby is born?"

Finally. The question she'd been waiting for. No, the question she'd been dreading, and one she couldn't answer. How could she tell him what she planned to do once the baby was born when so much of her decision depended on him?

She pulled the cereal bowl toward her and took a bite, postponing the inevitable. Sipping her tea, then cradling the mug to her chest, she sat back in her chair. "Tell me about Tyler and Jud. What's been going on on the ranch?"

"Tyler's fine. Jud's fine. The ranch is fine."

"But you're not."

"I'm sorry, Harley. It's just that we left a lot unsettled a month ago because we both needed time." He looked up. Emotion darkened his eyes. "Time's run out."

"No, Gardner. Time has just begun. You've only had three or four hours to deal with this. We can talk about it once you've thought it through. And once I'm feeling better. While you're here, I want to enjoy the time we have." She reached out and laid one hand along his jaw. "Please, please don't press me about this."

He gave in then, grudgingly, but she could see it in his eyes. She'd bought herself some time, nothing more.

"Now, unless you're really in the mood for your own bowl of Cream of Wheat, why don't you go get something to eat? If you tell me what you're in the mood for, I can tell you where to go."

He looked uncertain, so she added, "I'll be fine. And we can talk when you get back."

"I'll go get a burger at the drive-through down the street." Gardner got to his feet. "Do you need anything while I'm out?"

"No, I'm fine. I think I'll curl up in bed and read for a while." She nodded toward her cereal bowl. "You know, give that gourmet meal a chance to settle."

"Where do you keep your extra pillows and blankets?"

"Why?"

Awkwardly, he inclined his head toward her living room. "If you're asleep when I get back, I'll sack out on the couch."

"No." This she knew for a fact. "I want you to sleep with me. I promise not to repeat my earlier performance."

"That's not what I'm worried about," he murmured, carrying her dishes to the sink.

"You think sleeping in the same bed with my sunken cheeks and bloodshot eyes might keep you awake?" she asked, injecting what humor she could into the grim moment.

He gave her an indignant glare. "I don't want to hurt the baby."

"Gardner, the baby's hardly big enough to be hurt. Please," she begged, then shamelessly added, "I could use some cuddling. Maybe a little more TLC."

After he'd cleaned up the kitchen, he finally agreed, leaving Harley in bed, snuggled back against a mountain of pillows, quilt tucked to her chin, paperback romance in hand.

But once he was gone, the door secure behind him, the room quiet and still, the printed words blurred together, until Harley had to blink to clear her vision.

Even then, she saw only Gardner's face, the unfathomable expression in his eyes. Confusion. Indecision. And the one thing she hadn't seen. The very thing she'd expected. Joy.

She told herself he needed time, that her revelation had come as a shock. Neither argument settled the butterflies in her stomach.

From day one Gardner had talked about children. His legacy. His heritage. He'd spoken in terms of the future, his words flavored with passion and the essence of love.

Love. An emotion he verbally denied, yet gave of so freely. An emotion she verbally demanded, but had yet to declare in return. It was time she set things straight.

Eyes closed, she allowed her mind to drift, waiting for Gardner to return, imagining him in bed beside her, picturing his body loving hers. Slipping from the bed, she lit the half-dozen beeswax candles hanging in sconces on the walls and a second dozen scattered around her dressing table.

She flicked off the lamp and crawled back in bed, naked. Waiting. Wanting.

When Gardner slid under the covers beside her later, she forced herself to relax, to take things slow. To ease into a discussion of their future, to turn the conversation to love.

He never gave her the chance. He pulled her bare back against his bare front, cupped one breast and laid a hand on her belly.

"A baby," he whispered, his fingertips rubbing low, lazy circles beneath her navel. "God, I've waited so long for this."

Harley shut her eyes on silent tears and willed the sensations building low and center beneath Gardner's hand to slow. Right now, his words took precedence over his touch, no matter the way she ached.

He blew a soft sigh against her ear. "When Tyler was born, I resented him for a long time. Not because he stole my parents' attention. Hell, I hadn't had that for years. But I didn't want a baby, I wanted a brother. For me."

He tensed; his hand stopped and Harley held her breath.

"By the time he was old enough to play with, though, I'd changed my mind."

"You didn't want a brother?" she asked.

"No. I wished he had never been born."

Harley's eyes flew open. "Gardner!"

"Face it, Harley. Some people should never have children. My parents, for example. Half of the time I don't think they remembered Tyler and I existed." His voice darkened. "He deserved better."

"So did you," Harley whispered, aching for those two small boys.

"Yeah, well." He shifted against her. "I couldn't think about that. It was bad enough watching the way they treated Tyler.

"The first time it happened he wasn't very old. His crying woke me up. He must've been going at it awhile because he was hysterical. When I went into his room he was on his knees in his crib. His head was stuck between two slats. He'd knocked his bottle out on the floor."

Gardner's body stiffened; the muscles in his legs bunched against the backs of her thighs. Harley settled into the curve of his body, pulling him around her, telling him she was there.

He hugged her as though he'd die if he didn't. "My parents were so busy grunting and banging, they didn't even hear Tyler cry. Hell, he was just a baby. A baby, for God's sake.

"After that I made sure he was taken care of." He splayed his fingers over her stomach, then lower, seeking the heat between her thighs. "You can be damned sure I'll take care of this one, too."

And you'll give your child all the love you have stored up inside, Harley thought. *All the love you've never been allowed to give.*

She started to turn, but he stopped her with the press of his broad shoulder. She glanced back, and he took her mouth, his kiss a devouring search before he buried his face in her neck.

His erection stirred against her bottom. He pulled his tongue from her mouth only long enough to ask, "You sure this is okay?"

Lying on her side, she nodded. Anticipation stole her breath. She was born for this man. And just as intuitively she knew that he loved her. She could wait to hear the words. What she couldn't wait for another moment was his body.

Holding the back of her thigh, Gardner lifted her leg, opening her body with one finger, then two. He spread her wide, pulled back his hand and came home.

"Hold on," he breathed against her neck and Harley felt his entry with her body and her soul. She wanted to cry with the pleasure.

He filled her, he fed her; their mutual hunger began with desire but deepened into the rare touch of souls. The intensity of his possession burned sharp and sweet. Her breathing came in jerky gasps and Gardner smiled against her skin.

"Good?" he asked through the tiny nips he was taking along her shoulder.

"Good," she managed, her neck arched, her fingers digging into the arm he had wrapped around her middle.

He thrust again and Harley whimpered. When she came, she took him with her. And when he would have eased from her body, she refused.

He'd been alone and unloved too much of his life already.

12

"HOW SOON CAN WE get married?"

"That has to be about the dullest proposal I've ever heard, Gardner Barnes," Harley said, snuggling closer to the most unromantically romantic man she knew.

"We've done this whole thing wrong from day one." He pulled her tightly into the crook of his arm and dropped a kiss on her head. "Why fix it now?"

"You're right. It has been strange," Harley said, thinking of the phone calls, the week she'd spent at the ranch with a man she didn't know. She'd known he would ask, no, demand they get married as soon as he found out about the baby. Still . . . "I'm not sure marriage at this point is the answer.

"Think about it, Gardner. Unmarried parents who get along and provide emotional stability are better than married parents with different goals and different outlooks on life, who can't agree, who end up fighting, end up hurting each other. And hurting their child."

"What makes you think we'd fight? And what makes you think our goals are so different?"

"That's not what I'm saying." Though she knew in essence it was.

Gardner trapped her leg beneath his. "Do people usually go into marriage with all their problems resolved?"

"I don't know about other people, Gardner. But I do know about us." She plucked at the silky fine hairs on his chest, circled one nail around his nipple. "Remember that day in your attic, Gardner. We talked about loving a child and the emotional commitment it takes to raise a family."

He gripped her hand, holding her still. "I would always be there for my child, Harley. Always. But being there emotionally is tough to do if I'm not there physically. That's why I want us to get married."

Not exactly what she'd wanted to hear, but... "Gardner—"

He laid two fingers over her lips. "You can make whatever arrangements you want. A justice of the peace works for me. Or we can get married in that little chapel where you worship. You don't have to move out to the ranch right away. I know you'll need time to settle things here. Hell, I'll buy the store and Mona—"

"Wait a minute, Gardner." Harley cut him off and leaned across him to flip on the bedside lamp, ignoring the brush of her nipples over his chest hair. She scooted up against the headboard, pillow hugged to her chest, hiding her nakedness—from what, she didn't yet know. "How do you know about the chapel where I worship?"

His eyes were sad, his expression guilty, and Harley's chill settled bone deep. "Tell me, Gardner."

"It was a long time ago. When we first met."

She arched one brow. "You mean last month."

One corner of his mouth slanted up, and he quietly said, "It seems like I've known you forever."

"Well, you haven't," she retorted. "And I've never told you where, or even if, I go to church." He fixed her with a steady look and Harley said no to the urge to back down.

"There were a lot of things I didn't know about you at first, Harley. A lot of things I wondered about because of what you did tell me. About your unconventional friends. The fact that your parents were bikers."

"And you wondered who I really was."

He nodded, shifting to sit higher.

Harley plowed on. "You wondered if I was suitable, worthy to be the mother of your children."

The sheet dipped dangerously low on his lap. "It was a business decision. One made before I knew you."

"You had me investigated." Her words fell flat. And when he didn't defend himself further, Harley's temper shot off the scale.

"Is that right, Gardner? Did you look into my past? Into my habits? Into my finances, the same way you would any asset you intended to acquire for Camelot? Did you check out my pedigree, too? Isn't that how you've built up King's herd?"

Hell had no fury like a woman scorned and Harley was just getting started. "Did you get as many cheap thrills checking up on me as you did having phone sex?"

The fire in Gardner's eyes burned bright. "Stop it, Harley."

"I don't want to stop, Gardner. Not when I've finally realized you were serious when you said you didn't believe in love. That all you wanted from me was children. I'm surprised you didn't just about gag on that marriage proposal." Nausea rolled in, and she pressed her fingers to the base of her throat.

"If I didn't want you, Harley, I wouldn't have asked."

Harley tossed her head, scraping the flyaway hair from her face. "Oh, yeah, you want me. In your bed. Or in my bed. Or in the bed in Fredericksburg. Or on the ground in broad daylight. Or in the back of the Rover.

"Let me ask you a question, Gardner. What would have happened if we'd met conventionally? If you had courted me, married me and then found out I couldn't have children. Would you have divorced me?"

He didn't answer and that broke Harley's heart. And to think she'd almost told him that she loved him. "Get out of my bed, Gardner. And then get out of my house. I won't kick you out of my life, because my baby deserves a father.

"But I will never marry you under any terms but my own. And until you can accept that, we have nothing more to say to each other."

"DAMMIT, GARDNER," Tyler said, stomping headlong down the center of the barn. "You cinch Merlin up any tighter you're gonna be saying howdy to this morning's oats."

Gardner unhooked the stirrup from the saddle horn and flipped it down. "He tries it and I know a dog or two that won't go hungry for a year. I've been puked on once too often this month."

"Bogie's is not the most reputable place to hang out, big brother." Tyler pitched a fork of clean straw into Merlin's stall. "Considering the bar's reputation, you've gotta figure you're going to run into a few sick-on-their-ugly-ass drunks."

Tyler couldn't know Gardner had been thinking about Harley, or that he couldn't spend enough time in the bar to forget her. Not that he wanted to, any more than he wanted to fight for custody of his baby. But he would.

He glared at his little brother. "What do you know about Bogie's reputation?"

"You know, Gardner," Tyler began, ignoring Gardner's reprimand. "The only other time I've seen you drunk is when Dad died."

Gardner didn't like the turn this conversation had taken. "So?"

"So you've had a burr up your butt since you got back from Houston. And I know for a fact that's where Harley lives."

"So?" Gardner growled louder.

"So I was thinking maybe you saw her, and maybe things didn't turn out the way you wanted." Pitchfork tongs down on the barn floor, Tyler stacked his fists on the handle. "Maybe that's the reason you've been putting in long hours at Bogie's instead of out on the range."

"If I'm drinking, it's my business," Gardner said, pulling Merlin's forelock free of the bridle, then adjusting the cheekstrap.

"It would be except for what happened to Jud." Tyler straightened, his tone of voice one hundred percent adult. "I'm not going to let it happen to you."

Ready to mount and get the hell out, Gardner locked his fist in a death grip on the saddle horn. "Let me worry about me, little brother."

"I can't. Not anymore." Tyler took a step forward and seized Gardner's wrist. "You've been my father since I was ten. It's time to be my brother and get on with your life."

"I like my life just fine."

"Gardner, you don't even have a life," Tyler said, stepping back and shoving the pitchfork against the barn wall. He gestured with a wide sweep of his arm. "You're up at dawn, out on the range until way past dark. You've lived, slept and breathed this ranch as long as I can remember. At least until the past couple of weeks. Is it Harley, Gardner? Is something wrong with Harley?"

Gardner couldn't help the twitch at the corner of his mouth. "Harley's pregnant."

Tyler's eyes widened, then narrowed. The look on his face switched from pleased to puzzled. "Then what the hell is she still doing in Houston?"

"She kicked me out."

Tyler's eyes narrowed insultingly. "What did you do?"

"Why would you think I did anything?"

"Because I've known you for eighteen years."

"Yeah, well, Harley's not like the women who grow up out here, Tyler."

"So I noticed."

"Yeah. And I noticed you noticing."

"Hey. What can I say. I'm enjoying the hell out of my prime." Thumbs in his belt loops, Tyler rocked back on his heels. "The women around here are real appreciative of that fact. And I gotta tell you, Gardner. They're real appreciative of you, too."

"Oh, yeah?" Gardner couldn't care less.

"Oh, yeah. There's been a lot of talk since you've been hanging out at Bogie's. They're figuring it was a woman that drove you there. And they're taking bets on who's gonna be the one to mend your broken heart."

"Fat chance."

"So it is broken."

Gardner shrugged.

"Then tell me what you did and tell me what you want to do about it. I'll give you some advice."

Gardner rolled his eyes. Just what he needed. Advice from Stud Central. "I had Harley investigated."

"*What?*"

Ignoring Tyler's openmouthed stare, Gardner grabbed Merlin's reins and headed out of the barn. "C'mon, Tyler. She eats tofu for Christmas and her parents are bikers. I didn't want the mother of my children to turn out to be a drug addict."

"Gardner, you're so stupid sometimes. One of these days you're gonna have to quit thinking with the head on your shoulders and do what the rest of us do."

"Thanks for the biology lesson, but I don't have time for what most people do."

"Harley isn't worth it?"

"Yeah, she's worth it."

"Then I give you permission—no, I order you to ease off. Take some time, Gardner. I can do more around the ranch."

"What about your finals?"

"Hey, I'll work it out. You've given up a lot of years, and a hell of a lot of personal hours. I think it's time I did the same in return. You know—" Tyler gave him an all-knowing Stud Central look "—before you get any older."

Gardner swung up into the saddle. Damn he loved this kid. "You know, Tyler, you've grown into some kind of man."

Tyler shrugged and stuffed his fists in the front pockets of his jeans. "I had a great teacher. Now what are you going to do about Harley?"

"I don't know."

"Do you love her, man?"

Gardner looked away. He closed his eyes and clenched his fists around the reins. Finally, he expelled a huge breath, turned and looked Tyler straight in the eye. "Yeah, I love her."

"Then tell her. What are you waiting for?"

Gardner looked at his too-smart-for-his-own-good little brother. He shook his head, a wry grin pulling at his mouth. "Don't worry about hauling the new pump out to Acre 52. I'll do it later."

"Uh-uh. I'll do it. You've got enough on your mind right now. Now get out of here," Tyler said and slapped Merlin on the rump.

The gelding surged forward in a tireless, ground-eating lope. Gardner settled his rump and moved with the horse. The motion was instinctive and left his mind free to wander.

He hoped his own child turned out as well as Tyler. The boy had a man's head on his shoulders. And he sure as hell asked hard questions.

What *was* he going to do about Harley?

He hadn't even bothered to explain that until he'd seen the report he'd forgotten about the investigation. That's how thoroughly she'd captivated him. Not that it made what he'd done right, but it was all he'd known to do at the time.

Camelot had been his life's obsession. He hadn't wanted to follow in his father's footsteps, but to bury them beneath his size-eleven Tony Lama's. To do things the way they needed to be done. And do them without losing himself in a woman to the point of forgetting who he was.

Taking that chance scared the hell out of him, and had kept him running when the wanting dug deep. He'd done what he'd set out to do. He'd taken care of his baby brother, and Tyler had come through the fires a fine young man. He'd taken care of Camelot, and the ranch would now pay him back.

When it had come time to take care of himself, to reward his effort with the children he so wanted, his search for their mother had proved fruitless. Until he met Harley.

Merlin snorted, and Gardner realized the horse had stopped at the crest of a sharp rise. The range spread out before him, scrub brush and mesquite and grassland without end. Camelot. His life. His mistress.

What he felt for the land now was nothing compared to his feelings for Harley. Her question before she'd booted him out left him speechless. He'd never considered the possibility of no kids, but the possibility of no Harley left his soul dead. He'd rather live childless with Harley than have a houseful of kids with anyone else.

As much as she was his weakness, she was also his strength. He was not his father. His love was as boundless as the Texas sky, big enough to cover Harley and as many kids as she would give him. She was carrying his child, and he didn't want to raise this child alone. He had to prove that he'd let go of his past and was ready to throw himself into the future.

And he thought he knew just how to do it.

SHE'D LOST twelve pounds. Seven weeks pregnant and
she'd lost twelve pounds. Ignoring the ledger spread
open on her desk, Harley reached for the calculator and
punched in the numbers. Not good. At her current rate
of weight loss, she'd weigh less than the baby when it
was born.

Ripping off the telltale tape, she stared down at the
black-and-red truth. She'd worried forever about bal-
ancing a demanding career and motherhood. It had
never occurred to her that she might fail before she'd
begun.

Of course, the doctor assured her that these hor-
mones run amuck signaled that her body was doing
exactly what it should to nourish a healthy fetus. She
wondered if Gardner would consider *that* evidence before he filed for custody.

She'd told him she'd take care of the baby. But the
look in his eyes when he'd walked out that night left no
doubt in her mind that he wanted this child—enough
so to make sure he got it.

Well, she hoped he was ready for a hell of a fight be-
cause he'd have one on his hands. This was her baby.
Her unconditional love. Her only remaining link to
Gardner. She'd be damned if he'd take any of that away.

A hysterical giggle bubbled up her throat. She was
damned anyway. Damned to love the man forever. The
man who would never love her. She'd wanted so much
to heal him, to show him that a consuming love need
not be destructive.

She'd showed him instead how unforgiving she was,
how selfish she was, how demanding. She'd listened to
him explain the investigation, but she hadn't heard a
word he said. Or more important, she'd heard the

words he hadn't said. That he didn't find her worthy. And she'd lived through that with Brad.

She understood his reluctance to give away any part of himself. He'd grown up in an unhealthy environment much as she had, but they'd responded differently, so differently. And that she chalked up to life.

But now that there was a child involved, the issue of love was more than nonnegotiable. It was set in sacred stone. This might not be the situation she'd dreamed of for her child, but she'd make it work. If she could survive this morning sickness, she could do anything. And she could do it alone.

"Delivery time." Mona placed the white cardboard box on the center of Harley's desk, on top of the ledger, six inches from Harley's face. The distinctive purple-and-orange striping blended together into a color Harley's stomach didn't want to think about.

She waved her hand. "Put it in the alcove with the ones from yesterday. Maybe I'll get to them tomorrow."

"You'll get to this one today."

"I may look like death on the hoof, but I still run this joint," Harley groused, sweeping a tangle of hair from her face. "Now I've got to get back to Dr. Fischer's account, if you don't mind."

"I do mind." Mona crossed impervious arms over her chest and ignored Harley completely. "This box will not wait."

"That's your opinion," Harley grumbled, nudging the box with the eraser end of her pencil. "It's not something that will spoil, is it? I can't take any more bad smells."

"It's from Camelot."

Harley's pencil clattered to the floor. Not now. Not when she'd finally managed her first tear-free day since telling Gardner to take a hike. Hesitantly, she laid one palm on the side of the box.

"So open it already." Mona shifted from foot to foot in her brown oxford flats. The hunter green and navy pleats of her skirt swished across the cuffed tops of her white socks.

"I think I'll take this one upstairs."

"No, you won't." At Mona's command, Harley shot her a quelling glance. Mona responded with a drill-sergeant look of her own. "I'll take it upstairs for you."

"You're a good kid, no matter what I say about you," Harley said, following Mona as she headed for the stairs.

"Is that kid remark a subtle slam of my choice of dress?"

Harley took another stair, glancing ahead of her at the navy cardigan skimming Mona's slim hips, pleated skirt and white socks. "Somehow, Mona, demure uni-formed schoolgirl doesn't suit you at all. You've got way too much sauce, spunk and sass."

"I went to an all-girls' school, you know," Mona said, nudging open Harley's front door with her hip. "I used to love to go to the dean's office. In fact, I made sure I was very naughty at least once every three or four weeks. At least until my final month."

"What happened?" Harley wasn't sure she wanted to know.

"The old dean retired. The new dean turned out to be a woman."

Harley couldn't even think to respond. She just rolled her eyes, following Mona into the living room. When

Mona lifted her shoulders in a questioning shrug, Harley said, "Take it to the bedroom. Just set it on my bed."

She waited until she heard the lock click into place and Mona's shoes scuff to the bottom of the staircase. Even then she could only stare at the box, wondering what Gardner had sent her. Wondering if she'd left something at the ranch and he'd returned it so he wouldn't have to think about her again.

Lord, her head hurt. Her stomach hurt. And her heart still wasn't through breaking.

Finally, not knowing got the better of her. The box wasn't heavy, it made only a slight indentation on her quilt. She knelt carefully before it, scissors in hand, and eased one long blade beneath the length of brown tape. One by one, she lifted the flaps, eased away the packing tissue and, breath held, peered inside.

It was Gardner's albatross, his anchor, the weight chaining him to the past. Slowly, reverently, Harley lifted his great-grandmother's wedding gown from the box and spread it over her bed. The Parisian lace had yellowed with age, as had the ivory satin and tulle. But the symbolism, the significance, the sense of love beyond life—none of that had dulled.

Blinking back tears, Harley reached into the box once more. Gardner's great-grandfather's medical kit, filled with priceless equipment and a lifetime of sacrifice. The man had left his family, removed himself from position and wealth, for the woman he loved.

Unable to do more than move through mechanical motions, Harley pushed the box to the floor. Hugging her knees to her chest, she rocked back and forth. She couldn't take any more. When would their hurting stop?

What had Gardner suffered to break this bond? He
was giving her his past and, by doing so, putting his
future in her hands. His actions were so much louder
than the words he didn't say. This gesture screamed his
love from the top of his lungs.

Silent tears rolled down her cheeks. She swiped them
away and reached for the tissue box on the table beside
her bed. And that's when she saw the note. A single
sheet of folded white paper that must have fluttered to
the floor.

His handwriting was scrawled but legible.

You alone are my life.
Yesterday, tomorrow and today.
From this day forward, from this day past.
All my worldly goods I thee endow.

GARDNER WAS HAVING a hell of a time figuring out Jud's
emergency. "Get on down to the pond and you'll see
what I'm talking about," didn't explain much at all. But
Gardner was in the Range Rover on his way to the
pond.

And from there he could head out to the south sixty,
and make one more check of the fence over Little Creek
before Sam Coltrain moved his herd into the pasture.

The money from the lease was going straight into
Tyler's college fund instead of winter feed. Tyler didn't
know it, but that was Gardner's prerogative. And more
than ever he intended to see to his brother's future.
Family was too important to take a back seat to business.

He owed his brother a lot. If not for Tyler's interference, he probably would have gone on being as hardheaded as always, refusing to admit what he felt for Harley was never going to go away.

Funny thing, but he was managing to work around it. The gnawing was always there, the hunger, the need to feel her fingers on his skin, and a load of her common sense upside his head. But he was managing just fine.

His childhood would forever be a part of who he was, but that was history. Living in the present had a hell of a lot more appeal, especially with Harley beside him. He wanted her beside him for the rest of his life, and had told her so by bundling up the past.

He hadn't called since sending her the package, wanting his gesture to speak for itself. Now all he had to do was wait. But he wouldn't wait long.

His cellular phone interrupted his musings. With a jerk of the wheel, he swerved to dodge a stump, and lifted the phone from its sleeve. "What now, Jud?"

"Do you think we could build a treehouse in the pecan tree by the pond?"

It was Harley. Harley. Harley wanted a treehouse in the pecan tree by the pond.

Jud and his damned emergency. He was going to wring his uncle's neck for this. And Tyler would just have to deal with another set of busted shocks. Gardner floored it.

"Gardner?"

What had she said? "A treehouse. Sure. How many stories?"

"I always wanted one of those Swiss Family Robinson things," she said, her voice resonant with the innocence he loved.

"That might be a little too much for one kid," he said, searching for casual conversation while he drove the hell out of the Ranger.

"Who said there's going to be just one kid?"

Gardner jammed on the brakes. He was having a heart attack. Right here. Right now. He wasn't even going to live to see his kids. "You mean twins?"

"No, silly. I mean one now, one next year, one the year after. As long as you pitch in and help."

"Oh, I'll pitch in." He launched the Rover back into motion.

Harley went on as if he hadn't said a word. "I mean, you didn't have a bit of trouble making yourself at home in my apartment. And being handy around the house is just one of the requirements I have for my husband."

Husband. Gardner couldn't breathe. Damn this game. "What are you saying, Harley?"

"I've already talked to Mona about the store. She wants it, and since she doesn't need the second floor for living space, she's going to put in a boutique." Harley sighed. "I think she's going to call it something like Moods, by Mona."

Gardner thought Mayhem might be a better choice, but he wasn't about to get into a discussion that wasn't important. Where was the damned pond?

"I'd also like for my husband to leave his work at the office. Considering we'll be living at the office, I realize that'll be hard."

Great. The pecan tree appeared over the top of the rise ahead. Down one more hill and . . . "Don't worry. I've just made it clear to both Tyler and Jud that I'm going to be backing off. I decided I want to enjoy what's left of my life."

"Good. I don't want a husband who's going to work himself into the ground."

"Well, that's taken care of. Any other requirements?"

"He has to be good in bed, but that's not a problem."

"Anything else?" Gardner asked, his voice husky with need and want and so much more. Finally, finally, there she was, her blond hair catching all the fire of the sun.

She glanced his way as he rolled toward her. "The most important thing. Between those children and that job, he's got to remember that I still need a whole lot of attention."

He jerked the Range Rover to a stop and got out. His heart wedged in his chest as he stared at Harley sitting cross-legged on the ground beneath the spreading pecan. His tree. His children's tree.

"That's easy. My wife is my number-one priority in life." He tossed the phone onto the dash, decisively strode across the firm ground and drew her to her feet. Her phone fell to the ground. "Now come here, wife."

"What are you doing?" she shrieked when he lifted her cotton T-shirt and tugged down the elastic waistband of her leggings.

He didn't answer, but yanked his own shirt free from his jeans, unbuckled his belt and spread open his fly. Then he pulled her to him, and rubbed her gently rounded pregnant belly over his. She was warm. She was Harley. And she was going to be his wife.

He pressed against her, the curve of her stomach the sweetest shape in the world. A baby. Their baby. God, he was going to die from happiness.

He kissed her then, sealing their pact, and starting a fire that she knew would last a lifetime.

Finally, after he'd tasted her mouth, her jaw, the slope of her shoulder and the length of her neck, Harley broke away.

"Gardner, are those my panties hanging from your rearview mirror?"

"Why?" he purred into her ear. "You want 'em back?"

"Nope. Never. And that's a very, very, very long time."

"Ah, Harley." He hugged her as close as two people could get and said the words that set him free. "I love you."

MILLION DOLLAR SWEEPSTAKES

UNLOCK THE DOOR TO GREAT ROMANCE AT BRIDE'S BAY RESORT

Join Harlequin's new across-the-lines series, set in an exclusive hotel on an island off the coast of South Carolina.

Seven of your favorite authors will bring you exciting stories about fascinating heroes and heroines discovering love at Bride's Bay Resort.

Look for these fabulous stories coming to a store near you beginning in January 1996.

Harlequin American Romance #613 in January
Matchmaking Baby by Cathy Gillen Thacker

Harlequin Presents #1794 in February
Indiscretions by Robyn Donald

Harlequin Intrigue #362 in March
Love and Lies by Dawn Stewardson

Harlequin Romance #3404 in April
Make Believe Engagement by Day Leclaire

Harlequin Temptation #588 in May
Stranger in the Night by Roseanne Williams

Harlequin Superromance #695 in June
Married to a Stranger by Connie Bennett

Harlequin Historicals #324 in July
Dulcie's Gift by Ruth Langan

Visit Bride's Bay Resort each month wherever Harlequin books are sold.

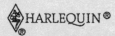

Mail Order Men—Satisfaction Guaranteed!

Texas Man—Tanner Jones

This rugged construction worker is six feet tall, with brown hair and blue eyes. His ideal woman is one who values love, trust and honesty above possessions.

Tanner Jones seems to be the answer to Dori Fitzpatrick's prayers. Ever since her rich ex-husband took her five-year-old son away from her, Dori's been looking for a way to get little Jimmy back. And she needs a husband to do it—preferably one who works for a living. But Dori soon finds out there's more to Tanner than meets the eye.

#600 HOLDING OUT FOR A HERO
by Vicki Lewis Thompson

Available in August wherever
Harlequin books are sold.

MMEN

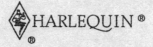

Sabrina   It Happened One Night
Working Girl   Pretty Woman
While You Were Sleeping

If you adore romantic comedies then have
we got the books for you!

Beginning in **August 1996** head to your
favorite retail outlet for
LOVE & LAUGHTER™,
a brand-new series with two books every
month capturing the lighter side of love.

You'll enjoy humorous love stories by favorite
authors and brand-new writers, including
JoAnn Ross, Lori Copeland, Jennifer Crusie,
Kasey Michaels, and many more!

As an added bonus—with the retail purchase,
of two new Love & Laughter books you can
receive a **free** copy of our fabulous
Love and Laughter collector's edition.

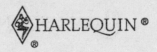

LOVE & LAUGHTER™—a natural
combination...always
romantic...always entertaining

◆ HARLEQUIN ®
®

A baby was the last thing they were

EXPECTING!

But after nine months, the idea of fatherhood begins to grow on three would-be bachelors.

Enjoy three complete stories by some of your favorite authors—all in one special collection!

THE STUD by Barbara Delinsky
A QUESTION OF PRIDE by Michelle Reid
A LITTLE MAGIC by Rita Clay Estrada

Available this July wherever books are sold.

HARLEQUIN ®

HREQ796

You're About to Become a
Privileged
Woman

Reap the rewards of fabulous free gifts and benefits with proofs-of-purchase from Harlequin and Silhouette books

Pages & Privileges™

It's our way of thanking you for buying our books at your favorite retail stores.

Harlequin and Silhouette—
the most privileged readers in the world!

For more information about Harlequin and Silhouette's PAGES & PRIVILEGES program call the Pages & Privileges Benefits Desk: 1-503-794-2499

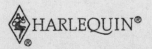

HARLEQUIN®

HT-PP152